The Irish Bedside Book

Edited By
JOHN M. FEEHAN

I0598030

THE MERCIER PRESS
CORK

Mercier Press
www.mercierpress.ie

This edition © the estate of John M. Feehan and individual authors

ISBN 978 1 78117 850 8

Transferred to digital print on demand in 2023.

Dedicated to Ulla Hammarborg

A CIP record for this title is available from the British Library

PREFACE

This anthology does not resemble any other that I know of and for that reason I feel it requires a few words of explanation.

With a few exceptions I have not included any of the well-known names in Irish literature because they have already appeared in most anthologies and I have a strong suspicion that the reading public have had their fill of them. Rather have I chosen little fragments of the hidden Ireland, amongst them gems far superior to anything written by their more renowned colleagues.

I have not inserted the names of the authors in the text because I think this only distracts the readers attention from the content of the piece. All the relevant names and other details are given in the sources at the end of the book.

This anthology is meant to be light, easy, pleasant reading with here and there the occasional deep and disturbing thought, and as its title suggest, it is something to be dipped into in those last relaxing moments before the day is done. I hope you enjoy it.

J.M.F.

ACKNOWLEDGEMENTS

The Editor would like to thank most sincerely the following for the use of copyright material: The Mercier Press and its various authors: John B. Keane, Eamon Kelly, James N. Healy, Patrick C. Power, Paddy Crosbie, Paddy Lysaght, Patrick Byrne, Padraic O'Farrell, Meda Ryan, Tomas de Bhaldraithe, Sean Og agus Manus O Baoill, Sean O Suilleabhain, Michael Keane, Eric Cross, Tony Baggot, Proinsias MacAonghusa, Riobard Breatnach and Maureen Joliffe. He would also like to thank Riobard O Farachain, Dr. Said Yasin, An Gum and the Executors of Daniel Corkery, Jimmy Young and Margaret Pearse. *Go mba fada buan iad.*

1. ETERNAL IRELAND

I am eternal Ireland – older than the hag of Bere
I had my hour of glory with Cuchulainn fair
I had my hour of sorrow, betrayed without a care
I am eternal Ireland, more lonesome than the hag
       of Bere.

2. LOVE SONG

O Máirín de Barra you have moidhered my thinking
And flooded the deep cup of pain for my drinking
From the held stare of silence at night I've no
       hiding
From the grief glare of morning, from sorrow's
       abiding.

I gave and I gave and I gave without stinting
On Candlemas Day in the church my heart's minting
For your eyes' smiling, grayer than corn-ears dew
       pearlings
And your mouth's singing, gayer than the dawn talk
       of starlings.

With wile I'd have won you, with kiss and with
       wooing
With wile I'd have won you, with silence and suing

With wile I'd have won you, when the barley was
        turning
But the blade was but sprung when you left me love
        mourning.

I envy the road that rings sweet to your treading
I envy the wind that your thyme-breath is wedding
I envy the pillow your sloe-head clouds over
And I envy to crazing of envy your lover.

I'd go and I'd go on through full lands and lonely
I'd rove over seas with no wealth but you only
If my clay the clay-quilt of the grave-bed lay under
And you said you were mine, I would rend earth
        assunder.

O Máirín you've made me the jest at the reaping
The tale of the market, the show for the peeping
The corn for the flailing of tongues at the threshing
The hound that the switch of their laughter is lashing.

3. ESSAYS

*The essays that follow have been taken from
Mucky Dunn's old copy book. Most of them were
written by Mucky himself; some however — those
given as homework — were the work of both
Mucky and his father. To make for easy reading
the spellings have been corrected.*

The reader may be puzzled by the final sentence in each short essay. Very clearly it has nothing whatever to do with the subject.

Most teachers would agree with me, when I say that a full page of copy is a satisfactory size for a normal essay in fifth or sixth. Coming towards the end of the writing exercise, however, a teacher notices that some boys have a couple of vacant lines to fill and with a few seconds to go, shouts: 'Come on now, fill those last couple of lines, quickly.' The boys, anxious to oblige, write in the first thing that comes into their heads.

Our Cat

Our cat wasn't always a cat; she used to be a kitten. Black cats are very lucky. Our cat is black and is very lucky. She ate my father's dinner on Saturday, while my mother was out.

Every night she is put out. Last Saturday night she was slung out by my father. She is a Manx cat. She used to be an ordinary cat until one night Mr Byrne slammed the door downstairs.

Her name is Twister and whenever we call her, everybody looks around. When we got her first, we called her Johnny. Last year my father brought her up to the canal to teach her how to swim but she managed to get out of the sack.

Dublin is the largest city in Ireland.

The Human body

Everybody has a body. It is made up of a head, a trunk and limbs. If you lose your arms, legs and head you still have a trunk, but if an elephant loses his head he loses his trunk as well. The head is the chief end of man. The brain is inside the head usually. A big head is not always a sign of brains because Snodser has the biggest head in our class. But big heads are very good for hiding behind. Eyes are for seeing with and ears are for holding up your glasses.

The head is nearly always covered with skin but it sticks out in one place. This is called a nose. Noses run in families. My father says that a red nose is caused by either sunshine or moonshine. I have heard of people who pay through the nose.

My aunt keeps hens.

Water

Water is the same colour as nothing; but it is much heavier and very wet. Rain is water broken into tiny bits. Everybody drinks water except my father.

Water is often disguised as snow, when it goes white with the cold. It runs down the walls in our house but our landlord says that that's sweat. I read in a book that steam is water gone mad with the heat! It very often goes stiff with the cold. This is called ice or hard water. A man who lives on water for a long time is called a sailor.

A man on TV said that water has no shape but he is wrong because it always fits our bucket. Snodser Quinn says that lemonade is sugary water that has got 'pins and needles'.

A bus is a very useful thing.

4. LOVE SONG

Believe me if all those endearing young charms
Which I gaze on so fondly today
Were to change by tomorrow and fleet in my arms
Like fairy gifts fading away
Thou wouldst still be adored as this moment thou art
Let thy loveliness fade as it will
And 'round the dear ruin each wish of my heart
Would entwine itself verdantly still.

It is not while beauty and youth are thine own
And thy cheeks unprofaned by a tear
That the fervour and faith of a soul can be known
To which time will but make thee more dear
Oh! The heart that has truly loved never forgets
But as truly loves on to the close,
As the sunflower turns on her God where he sets
The same look that she gave when he rose.

5. PRO PATRIA MORI

He was convinced that there were countries which
would come into the Empire if assured of defence.
To carry out such a scheme it would be necessary
to expel Southern Ireland.

6. FROM THE DOCK

Mr President and Gentlemen of the Court-Martial, I mean not to give you the trouble of bringing judicial proof to convict me legally of having acted in hostility to the government of his Britannic Majesty in Ireland. I admit the fact. From my earliest youth I have regarded the connection between Great Britain and Ireland as the curse of the Irish nation, and felt convinced that, whilst it lasted, this country could never be free nor happy. My mind has been confirmed in this opinion by the experience of every succeeding year, and the conclusions which I have drawn from every fact before my eyes. In consequence, I was determined to employ all the powers which my individual efforts could move, in order to separate the two countries. That Ireland was not able of herself to throw off the yoke, I knew; I therefore sought for aid wherever it was to be found. In honourable poverty I rejected offers which, to a man in my circumstances, might be considered highly advantageous. I remained faithful to what I thought the cause of my country, and sought in the French Republic an ally to rescue three million of my countrymen . . . .

7. TO A LINNET IN A CAGE

When Spring is in the fields that stained your wing,
    And the blue distance is alive with song,
And finny quiets of the gabbling spring
    Rock lilies red and long,
At dewy daybreak, I will set you free
    In ferny turnings of the woodbine lane,
Where faint-voiced echoes leave and cross in glee
    The hilly swollen plain.

In draughty houses you forget your tune,
    The modulator of the changing hours.
You want the wide air of the moody noon,
    And the slanting evening showers.
So I will loose you, and your song shall fall
    When morn is white upon the dewy pane,
Across my eyelids, and my soul recall
    From worlds of sleeping pain.

8. A SONG AT TWILIGHT

A matchmaker is a man or woman practised in the gentle art of creating permanent alliances between men and women who might otherwise never participate in that long drawn-out confrontation known as marriage. For a short while I acted in such a capacity but it was only because the local matchmaker had passed on to his eternal reward as the place beyond the grave is hopefully called. I was neither a success nor a failure but I can proudly say that I was responsible for two marriages. One of the couples is blissfully happy but neither of the others have spoken to me since the knot was permanently tied. The male of the partnership in particular has it in for me and I have the fearful feeling that he is constantly endeavouring to whip up sufficient courage for one redoubtable, all-out assault.

Small blame to him for I am told that his spouse is incapable of silence for more than a second at a time. He has not spoken to her for several years and when he was chided by his father-in-law for this long lapse in communications he countered by saying that he didn't like interrupting her.

After this I gave up matchmaking and would refer aspiring martyrs to marriage bureaux or to experienced matchmakers who presided over other districts. To my mind a matchmaker is not unlike a judge whose painful duty it sometimes is to pass heavy sentences on those who appear before him. It is inevitable that those convicted by him will bear him ill-will and malice. It is the same with a matchmaker. It is he who caused the marriage in the first place. If the liaison is happy all is well but if it is not he has passed a heavy sentence on two innocent people. They are not likely to forget him in a hurry. There are men I know who heartily detest the man or woman who first introduced them to the women who later became their wives. It is a thousand times worse in the case of a match-maker and there are some I know who walk warily, always on the look-out for retaliation.

Personally I look upon marriage as a game, a very long game, of course. There are ups and downs, moments of great elation and deep depression, indiscretions, bouts of temper and what-have-you.

It is a game which requires only two contestants and there is no need for an umpire or a referee. Once the whistle is blown there can be no outside interference, no stopping of the play until one of the principals is called off the pitch by his or her maker. That is the final whistle for the partner in question but not for the one left on the field of play. One may start a new game with a new partner if one so desires and provided a new partner is available.

It is unquestionably the oldest game in the world and even those who have been punished and pummelled by its sometime rigours would not swop it for any other game. The tragedy is that there are millions of prospective players standing in the sidelines most anxious to participate but lacking the drive to dash into the game.

Here is where the gentle art of matchmaking comes into its own. Your astute fixer of lasting partnerships will look for teams that are evenly matched. Since there is only one player on each team this is not as difficult as it first may seem. The object in selecting teams which are evenly matched is to ensure that decisive victory never goes to either side, that there is draw after draw and replay after replay. Thus only can a game that is satisfying to both teams be assured.

Physical resemblance has little to do with it for I

have often seen a seven-stone man outplay a fif-teen-stone woman and I have seen a woman of five feet outfield a man of six feet three.

Where there is marriage tardiness in a village or townland there is an absolute necessity for a matchmaker. Where people are retiring and shy and incapable of speaking for themselves the match-maker will do it for them. Maybe the result is not always heavenly bliss but a human voice is better than the four walls of an empty room, not to men-tion the cold of an empty bed.

Sometimes there are couples who have been courting for years but for one reason or another the vital question is never popped. Seasons pass and hair grows grey yet there is no suggestion that a marriage bed should be permanently shared. What is needed here is a prompt or a pinch or a push and the man best qualified to do this is your matchmaker.

I once heard of a couple who were walking out together for seven years but the male member of the firm never once hinted at marriage. Once when she said it would be nice to get married his reply was, 'who in God's name would marry the likes of us?' Not once did he give her a kiss or place an arm around her. One cold night they were sitting on a windy bridge when she complained of the cold.

'If my mother was here now,' said the girl, 'she'd put an arm around me to save me from the cold.'

'Now, now,' said the boyfriend, 'I can't be wak-ing up your mother at this hour of the night.'

This is the way with many a couple. Time passes them by. Their inability to take the plunge means that they must forego the thrills and spills of the greatest game known to man. That is why the art of matchmaking must never be allowed to die. It is a pauperised parish that cannot maintain or encourage one. We should all aspire to part-time matchmaking because the truth is that but for the matchmakers of yesterday many of us might not be here today.

9. TO BE IRISH

By God I know I'm Irish
Although I am a Prod.
I've come from Central Europe
But I've settled on the sod,
I've dug, I've worked, I've dreamt, I've cried,
I've tried to play my part.
For there's something strange in Ireland
That gets you, near the heart.

But we all have come from Europe
A few thousand years ago;
From somewhere in the Baltic
Or from far Himalyan snow,
Where thoughts were dreamed at leisure
Of something deep and true —
That's how I know I'm Irish
I know the things they knew.

Those things were thought at leisure
Before the world went mad,
And sold its soul for pots and pans
Forgetting what we had,
And now our stomach has grown big
Our heads grown very small
Just like the doubting dinosaur
Who isn't here at all —

We wonder where we're going,
We've forgotten where we were.
We have a funny feeling that we're getting very ill,
So we go to our psychiatrist
Or we take the bloody pill.

We need to walk beside the shore
And rest beside the sea,
And let its calm and healing strength
Tell us what we should be.
Then with some sense of urgency
Utter our lost identity.

Oh get up off your arse, you fool,
And leave the pill and chair
And walk in Ireland's holy land
— Breath unpolluted air.
Climb up the mystic mountains
And there, be still, and know
That honest sort of something
We all knew long ago.

10. ISLAND REVERIE

I sailed along quite close to the rocky cliffs of Cape Clear and passed a series of points and inlets with such wonderful and unusual names that they must have been thought up first day by a race of people steeped in rhythm and music: Tonenaginkeenee, Boilgeen, Reenrourbeg, Carrigancuraun, Coolvaw, Lehanaun, Coosangaslawk, Coosanglanierig, Coosnaboilge, Deedaunmuar, and many others. Indeed every place-name in Cape has the ring of song about it. In no time at all I came to the opening between Bream Point and Bullig Point, which leads into South Harbour, and exactly three hours and fifteen minutes out from Baltimore, I brought *Dualla* to a halt and dropped anchor in one-and-a-half fathoms of water so pure and clear that I could nearly see the hook biting it. After a quick light lunch I rowed ashore with Maxie, since, like us human beings, he had a little matter to attend to, and unlike as human beings he's not a bit ashamed to attend to it in public.

It was a delightful afternoon so I went for a long stroll up over the hills, past the little schoolhouse, towards the eastern end of the island. Compared with other European islands Clear is gradually reverting to a primitive condition – untilled fields, overgrown fences, ruined cottages – but perhaps that, and the freedom to wander at will without running up against *Verboten* notices, is what gives it its peculiar charm, and makes you want to return again and again. The island is teeming with rabbits who take little notice of passers-by and in nearly every field they sat in circles looking solemnly at each other like as if they were sitting in council deliberating on problems of great weight and import affecting the destiny of their world. Indeed they paid little or no attention to Maxie either, and I was delighted to see that he did not make the slightest attempt to chase them. Here we were on a dream island, wild animals, a tame animal and a human being respecting each other's rights and all enjoying to the full the peaceful, rapturous, summer's day. I wandered leisurely along the rugged path until I came to the cross roads at Killicknaforavane and here I swung back west, past the little chapel, towards Trá Kiaran and the North Harbour. There are not enough superlatives in the English language to describe the view from this elevated road; to the east Carbery and all its three hundred isles, to the North Mount Gabriel and the Kerry mountains peeping over its shoulder, to the west the Mizen, the Bull Lighthouse, and the majestic Fastnet, and traversing everything the heaving, restless sea. I paused for a moment to absorb it all but once again, 'the beauty of this world hath made me sad' – this tragic beauty, this sad song of human limitations. Keats, who was the great poet of melancholy and mortality, is my kindred spirit. He was vividly aware of the conflict between transcience and permanence, between sadness and joy, in every facet of human life. He saw so clearly what most human beings like to blot out of their minds that, 'all we have loved, or shall love, must die.' The price of all laughter and merriment is death. The almost beatific beauty of the Nightingale's song awakened in him feelings of melancholy:

Fade far away, dissolve and quite forget
What thou amongst the leaves hast never known
The weariness the fever and the fret
Here, where men sit and hear each other groan
Where palsy shares a few, sad, last grey hairs
Where youth grows pale, and spectre-thin and
*   dies,*
Where but to think is to be full of sorrow
And leaden-eyed despairs

11. PRIORITIES

Even the Council horse, a fine big-boned, well-fed animal, is now going about his work in the same lackadaisical fashion as the Council Employees.

12. BLIND POET

I am Raftery the rhymer
Full of hope and care
With the empty gape of blindness
Searching the silent air.

Travelling the same old roadways
With only the light of my heart
Weariness and tiredness
Pull body and soul apart.

Look at me now my fellows
With my back to the wall of the school
Trying to fiddle my music
To the empty pockets of fools.

13. NORTHERN INTERLUDE

I was born and bred in Sandy Row, a loyal Orange
    Prod,
A follower of King William, that noble man of God.
My motto 'No Surrender', my flag the Union Jack,
and every year I'd proudly march to Finaghy and
    back.
A loyal son of Ulster, a true blue that was me,
    prepared to fight, prepared to die, for faith and
    liberty.
As well as that a Linfield man as long as I could
    mind.
I had no time for Catholics, or people of that kind.
Then one night down in Bangor, I met wee Rosie
    Brown and from the minute I set eyes on her,
    my heart went up and down.
And when I thought she fancied me, my brain was
    all a buzz, and I clean forgot to ask her,

what her religion was.

I never slept a wink that night, I just lay there in
    bed;

I thought about wee Rosie and all the things she'd
    said.

I know I should have asked her sort, before I made
    a date, before I fell in love with her; but then it
    was too late.

When next we met I told her, I'm a Prod and
    staunch and true, and she said, 'I'm a Catholic,
    and just as staunch as you.'

The words were harsh and bitter, and then suddenly
    like this, the centuries of hatred were forgotten
    in one kiss.

That night I dreamt about her, a strange confusing
    dream, I dreamt we both were singing the
    'Wearing of the Green'.

And as we walked to Finaghy, full of harmony and
    hope, who was there to greet us but his holiness
    the Pope.

When I awoke, I knew that dream was even more
    than true, the future we were heading for would
    be confusing too.

Indeed, when I thought about it, it was all too clear

That that was to be the under statement of the year.

I knew our love could bring us little but trouble
    and distress, but nothing in this world could make
    me love my Rosie less.

I saved a bit of money as quickly as I could, and I
    asked her if she'd marry me, and by God she said
    she would.

Then the trouble really started, her folk were flam-
    ing mad, and when mine heard about it, sure,
    they were twice as bad.

Her father said that from that day he's hang his
head in shame, and by a strange coincidence, my
oul lad said the same.

My mother cried her eyes out, and said I would rue
the day

I would let a Papish hussy steal my loyal heart away.

Rosie's mother said, when she had recovered from
the blow, that she'd rather see the devil than
that man from Sandy Row.

In deference to Rosie, we were married in her
church, but my clergyman was there as well, he
didn't leave me in the lurch.

The priest was awful nice to me, he made me feel
at home, I think he pitied both of us, for you see
our families wouldn't come.

The house we went to live in had nothing but four
walls, it was far away from Sandy Row, and
further from the Falls,and that's the way we
wanted it, for both of us knew well that back
among the crowd we knew, our life would just
be hell.

But life out there for Rosie was lonely I well knew,
and of course we had our wee religious differences
too.

When Friday came along and Rosie gave me fish

I looked at it, and then at her, and I said, 'That's
not my dish.'

I mind well what she answered, though she never
said it twice, to eat no meat on Friday, is a poor
wee sacrifice to make for Christ who died for us,
one Friday long ago.

Anyway, I ate the fish, and it wasn't bad you know.

Then Sunday came and I lay on, and she got up for
Mass, and Rosie turns to me and says, 'Will you

shift your lazy ass? you've got a church to go to, and that's where you should be, so up you get this minute, you'll go part of the road with me.'

We left the house together, but we parted down the line, and she went off to her church and I went off to mine.

But all throughout the service, although we were apart, I felt I was worshipping, with Rosie in my heart.

The weeks and months went quickly by and then there comes a day, Rosie up and tells me that a child is on the way.

And from that very minute my life became a wondrous thing, like a lovely flower unfolding its petals in the Spring.

We wrote and told our families, for of course they never came to call, and we thought this news would help to heal the breach and so it did and all.

My mother and then Rosie's came to visit us in turn, and I marvelled at the power of a wee child yet unborn.

Och, but I was awful disillusioned when I found out why they came.

It wasn't just to heal the breach or make it up again
— ah no, Rosie's mother had come to say that the child had to be RC, and mine had come to say it had to be a Protestant like me.

The rows before the wedding were surely meek and mild, compared with all the rumpus that was ris about the child.

From both sides of the family insults and threats were hurled —

What a desperate way to welcome a wee angel to

this world.

The child must be a Catholic,' 'No the child must
be a Prod,' but the last and powerful voice I
heard, was the mighty voice of God, and to his
awful wisdom, I had to bow my head, when
Rosie's time had come at last, the child was born;
but dead.

That night I sat by Rosie's bed, and just before the
dawn

I kissed her as she left me, to join our angel son.

And this Orange heart was broken within these
four bare walls.

Where the hell's the Shankill? Where the hell's the
Falls?

In all the years that's past since then, the years of
grief and pain, I would give my life and even more,
just to see her face again.

But the loneliness is near over now, I'll see her soon
I know, for the doctor told me yesterday I
haven't long to go.

And when I go up thonder, they'll let me in I hope,
and if they ask me who I'm for, King William or
the Pope, I'm going to take no chances, I'll tell
them loud and clear, that I'm just a loyal Protestant that loved... A Papisher.

But one way or another, I think they'll let me
through, and Rosie will be waiting there with our
wee angel too

And then a child will lead them, the Papisher, and
the Prod, up the Golden steps of heaven, into
the house — of GOD.

14. DEATH

A Shiobhán bhocht, tá tú leagtha amach anois ag na mná, is tá eagla mo chroí orm go mbrisfidh mo shiúl do reast. Is tá amhras agam go bhfuil tú i ndúiche na socrachta anois, ach ní leagfaidh mise mo shúil go feirc mo shaoil arís ar éinne a ghearrfaidh an leac oighre mar tusa. Bhítheá ar aonach is ar mhargadh liom i m'fhochair, is amasa ní mar a lán ban eile é le d'chaidhp anuas ar do shúile, ach ba í a bhí socruithe go cumhag siar ar do chúl. Is maith is cuimhin liom an mhaidin a tháinig an fear beag san aneas leis an teanga bhlasta a shíl an dá laoín d'fháil uainn ar phort Mháire Bun ach, má shíl, chuir tusa an tine ina eireaball ag imeacht, is chuiris na deargnaidí ag preabarnaigh ar ghruaig an Chiarraígh. Agus is maith is cuimhin liom an mhaidin aonach na Nollag ar tháinig an sliúcaidéir eile acu ar lorg an mhuicín reamhair ar ghreim cealacan an asail ach, má tháinig, chuir tusa a oiread deithnis leis is a chuireadh leis an mBeistiunach Rua an lá a bhí sé a d'iarraidh a bhean a sracadh amach ó bhannda an rotha, nuair nach bhfaigheadh sí cos a chur fúithi le meisce, agus eagla a chroí air go mbeadh sé gafa ag na píléirí mar gheall ar a muineál a chur faoin roth é féin.

Níor tháinig mé isteach ón ngairdín riamh chugat nach raibh an geaitín oscailte, an t-asal friothálta is an scilléidín leitean i gcóir i leataobh ar an tine ach anois beidh an geaitín dúnta is an t-asal gan friothálamh is an scilléidín is a bhéal faoi leasmuigh den doras, agus ní bhéarfaidh tú ar an spiúin iarainn go bráth arís. Agus dá mbeadh éinne siar ar a roinnt ba é tú féin é, a bhean an chroí mhóir, is má rith an gabhar bán tirim ní raibh a fhios ag an gabhar dubh é. Sheinnfeá port ar do theanga is rincfeá é is, b'fhéidir, caisí ar do bholg ag an am céanna, is dá mbeadh bean eile i d'bhróga is minic nach mbeadh maireachtain an chait duibh an lá mharaigh sé francach gona fear. Nuair a thagadh an chomharsa leis an gcapall chun an gairdín a threabhadh duit théadh sé amach uait is a bholg i riocht scoilthe, tughthá prátaí is feoil ghuirt is cabáiste geal dó, is tughthá builín is tae is uibheacha lachan dó, is tughthá an cairtín leanna dó a thug tú leat chun a bheith i gcóir don lá a chuaigh tú go dtí an margadh. Bhuaileadh sé amach ansin go dtí na comharsain ag beiliseáil as, is deireadh sé gur aon fhear bocht go raibh bean mhaith rathúil aige go raibh a chearc ar an nead aige is a chíos ina phóca. Agus anois, a ghrághil bhoicht, caithfidh mé do lámh a chrothadh ar na nóiméid déanacha is ní mór gur thaobh thiar de m' dhroim é, mar tá na mná bochta anseo chun tú a shocrú go binn isteach i do chónra, is tá tú chomh néata is go mbeidh tú ag suirí go hard ar an saol eile. Agus chím a gcinn cromtha is an sileadh ag titim óna súile mar deir siad nach bhfeicfidh siad bean mar thusa i ndiaidh léine ghlain go bráth arís, mar níor stoithis ribe de ghruaig éinne riamh is marar líon tú an cupán níor dhoirt tú é. Ach chím an solas gorm anois ag soilsiú ort, is dá sháimhe a bhíomar riamh tá amhras agam go mbeidh tú míle uair níos saibhre 'ges na grásta anois, mar ní bheidh aon tochas ar t'aigne cá bhfaighidh tú do bhricfeasta maidin Domhnach Cásca. Socróidh na haingil leaba shámh duit, is ní ghá duit aon eagla a bheith ort go scuabfaidh aon

ghaoth an staicín eornan as cúinne an ghairdín go
bráth arís. Déanfaidh mé fíor na Croise ort anois
idir tú féin is an t-Áirseoir, is ní dhéanfaidh Dia thú
a iompú díreach ag ceann gach aon lána cam
isteach go dtí an Talamh Beannaithe stróinséartha,
an áit a bhfuil an fómhar gearrtha is buailte is an
scioból líonta suas go dtína barr leis an ngráinne
nach dteipfidh go bráth.

15. LOYALTY 1979

The Councillors of Kingstown, Co. Dublin, known
to some as Dun Laoghaire, have decided to remain
loyal to the memory of his late majesty, King
George IV. By a majority of eight votes to two
they decided not to honour Patrick Pearse in his
centenary year. There is reason to believe that this
is but the first outright refusal by a local authority
to rename a street after the 1916 leader.

Dun Laoghaire's Fine Gael and Labour
councillors joined together to defeat a motion by
Fianna Fail's Owen Hammond that George's Street
should become Pearse Street. Some may recall that
this action was forecast in this column some
months ago.

Feeling in the area is now running high,
especially among younger people, and some praise
Jane Dillon-Byrne of Labour who declined to go

along with Labour's attitude to Pearse but
abstained instead.

16. THE BRIDAL BED

It's a hard misfortune for a poor cold fellow
Who now is near the age of three twenties
With the curly-haired girl dried-up to lie
Without life or sweetness in his rod, only slime!
Do you now understand, oh fine decent people,
That 'twas madness and frenzy for a grey-haired
    creeper
To look for sex when his jaw is wrinkled
When a fellow of twenty could manage her simply.
And must it be thought that 'twas she that was
    guilty
Or else that he conquered his state of stiffness?
This well-made, handsome, grey-eyed lady —
'Tis certain she received a different training.
If the night was hard work, she wouldn't be weary
And return as good to a lively piercer.
In the race of three she never refused him,
On the flat of her back with her eyes occluded;
She wouldn't upset him by a sulky rage,
A cat's assault, a tear or a scrape,
But she would stretch out luxuriantly,
Bit by bit his thoughts seducing,
Side to side and her limbs around him,

Mouth on mouth, pawing him downwards.
Often around him she twined her foot;
From his belt to his knee her brush she rubbed;
She snatched from his loins the quilt and the
    blanket,
With a cheerless old heap to play and dally.
It's often she grasped his lifeless sceptre
And rubbed its mouth to her groin with frenzy,
Took it within her soft hand nimbly,
And roused not the wretch to excitement or
    business,
She often before him a fine flat-cake set,
A delicacy made of duck and hen-eggs
Milk warmed-up she used give him with butter
And kept on nagging until he had drunk it;
She might as well into the dung-heap have thrown
Or given to the collie who turns the sheep
    homeward
Than to a clot give it — a streelish old man,
Withered and vile without gaiety or laugh.

17. KILKENNY DAME

The Bishop of Ossory at the time was Richard de Ledrede, a Franciscan friar and English by birth. Hearing rumours of strange goings on he made a visitation of his diocese in 1324, and by means of an Inquisition, consisting of five Knights and several nobles found there was a bank of heretical sorcerers in the city, headed by Dame Alice. The Inquisition drew up the following charges:—

1. That the sorcerers had denied the faith of Christ absolutely for a year and a month, accordingly as the object they desired to gain through sorcery was of greater or lesser importance. During this period they believed in none of the doctrines of the Church; did not adore the Body of Christ, nor hear Mass, nor make use of consecrated bread or holy water.

2. They offered in sacrifice to demons living animals, which they dismembered, and then distributed at cross-roads to a certain evil spirit of low rank, named the Son of Art.

3. They sought by their sorceries advice and responses from demons.

4. In their nightly meetings they blasphemously imitated the power of the Church by fulminating sentence of ex-communication, with lighted candles, even against their own husbands.

5. In order to arouse feelings of love or hatred or to inflict death or disease on the bodies of the faithful, they made use of powders, unguents, ointments and candles of fat, which were compounded as follows: they took the entrails of cocks sacrificed to demons, certain horrible worms, various unspecified herbs, dead men's nails, the hair, brains and shreds of grave clothes of boys who were buried unbaptised with óther abominations, all of which were cooked, with various incantations, over a fire of oak logs in a vessel made out of the skull of a decapitated thief.

6. The children of Dame Alice's first three husbands accused her before the Bishop of having killed their fathers by sorcery, and of having enchanted them so that they left all the wealth to her and her favourite son, William Outlawe, to the impoverishment of the other children. They said her present husband (Sir John le Poer) had been reduced to such condition by sorcery and powders that he had become terribly emaciated, his nails had dropped off and there was no hair on his body. He would have died had he not been warned by a maidservant, in consequence of which he forcibly possessed himself of his wife's keys and had opened some chests in which he found a sackful of horrible and detestable things which he transmitted to the Bishop through the hands of two priests.

7. The Dame had a certain demon, an incubus named Art or Robin, son of Art, who had carnal knowledge of her, and from whom she admitted she had received all her wealth. This incubus made its appearance under various forms sometimes as a cat, as a hairy black dog or in the likeness of a Negro (Aethiops), accompanied by two others who were larger and taller than he, and of whom one carried an iron rod.

Another source said the sacrifice to evil spirits consisted of nine red cocks and nine peacock eyes. Dame Alice was also accused of having 'swept the streets of Kilkenny between compline and twilight, raking all the filth towards the doors of her son, William Outlawe, chanting:

> To the house of William my sonne,
> Hie all the wealth of Kilkenny town.'

18. IRELAND

I called you by sweet names by wood and linn,
You answered not because my voice was new,
And you were listening for the hounds of Finn
    And the long hosts of Lugh.

And so, I came unto a windy height
And cried my sorrow, but you heard no wind,
For you were listening to small ships in flight,
    And the wail on hills behind.

And then I left you wandering the war
Armed with will, from distant goal to goal,
To find you at the last free as of yore,
    Or die to save your soul.

And then you called to us from far and near
To bring your crown from out the deeps of time,
It is my grief your voice I couldn't hear
    In such a distant clime.

19. TINKERS

Because the traffic on the roads has grown;
Because the fumes pollute the little town;
Because the kids must learn how to compete
And must have shoes, not nature
To enclose their soft, brown feet.

I offered one small corner of a field
I called my own.
And tried to understand
The distant stare
In far away, hard, dark brown
Eyes of stone.

They settled and we lived,
One winter long,
In strained and distant
Solemn company.

The summer came, and they found wings
For that contraption of a caravan,
Bought by the contributions
Of well-meaning friends.

I stood and meditated in the field
Where all that now remained
Was one pale stream of light blue smoke
Curling its heavenward path
Above the vacant spot.

20. DAY BY DAY

February 27th, 1829: Maread (Peggy) St. John
came to me today to work for seven shillings a
quarter.

July 1st, 1829: Now at this moment, at eleven
o'clock at night my wife died, having received
Extreme Unction, by the will of God.

July 10th, 1831: Peggy St. John delivered of a
daughter today.

July 21st 1831: Peggy St. John and her young daughter left me today. I believe she will never come back.

February 9th, 1832: Peggy St. John broke four window panes in my house today.

September 28th, 1832: Nurse Moore gave up the child to Peggy St. John.

January 25th, 1834: Paid M. (Peggy) St. John up to January 25th.

April 27th, 1834: Spent the night very foolishly in the company of Tomas Toibin . . . and with M (Peggy) St. John. May it do me no good!

January 25th, 1835: Ellen Tracey came as a maid to me today at four shillings a quarter.

21. PASSED TO YOU

References in this Order to the region of a regional commissioner shall be construed as references to the region for which such regional commissioner is the regional commissioner.

22. VISION

Naked I saw you
O beauty of beauty
And I blinked my eyes
Lest I fail in my duty.

Your music I heard
O sweetest of sound
And my hearing I closed
Lest I totter aground.

I relished your lips
O sweetness of sweetness
And I braced up my heart
.For fear I'd be shroudless.

I blinded my eyes
And my ears I sealed
I braced up my heart
My desire I healed.

I turned my back
On my vision in space
To the road ahead
I turned my face

I have turned my face
To the road ahead
To the fight I forsee
And my end with the dead.

23. EASTER WEEK 1916

'Romantic Ireland's dead and gone,
    It's with O'Leary in the grave.'
Then, Yeats, what gave that Easter dawn
    A hue so radiantly brave?

There was a rain of blood that day,
    Red rain in gay blue April weather,
It blessed the earth till it gave birth
    To valour thick as blooms of heather.

Romantic Ireland never dies!
    O'Leary lies in fertile ground,
And songs and spears throughout the years
    Rise up where patriot graves are found.

Immortal patriots newly dead
    And ye that bled in bygone years,
What banners rise before your eyes?
    What is the tune that greets your ears?

The young Republic's banners smile
    For many a mile where troops convene,
O'Connell Street is loudly sweet
    With strains of Wearing of the Green.

The soil of Ireland throbs and glows
    With life that knows the hour is here
To strike again like Irishmen,
    For that which Irishmen hold dear.

Lord Edward leaves his resting place
    And Sarsfield's face is glad and fierce.
See Emmet leap from troubled sleep
    To grasp the hand of Padraic Pearse!

There is no rope can strangle song
    And not for long death takes his toll.
No prison bars can dim the stars
    Nor quicklime eat the living soul.

Romantic Ireland is not old.
    For years untold her youth will shine,
Her heart is fed on Heavenly bread,
    The blood of martyrs is her wine.

24. LAST WORDS

I, John Langley, born at Wincanton, in Somersetshire, and settled in Ireland in the year 1651, now in my right mind and wits, do make my will in my own handwriting. I do leave all my house, goods, and farm at Black Kettle of 253 acres to my son, commonly called 'Stubborn Jack', to him and his heirs for ever, provided he marries a Protestant, but not Alice Kenrick, who called me 'Oliver's whelp'. My new buckskin breeches and my silver tobacco stopper with 'J.L.' on the top I give to Richard Richards, my comrade, who helped me off at the storming of Clonmel when I was shot through the leg. My said son John shall keep my body above ground six days and six nights after I am dead; and Grace Kendrick shall lay me out, who shall have for so doing five shillings. My body shall be put upon the oak table in the brown room, and fifty Irishmen shall be invited to my wake and every one shall have two quarts of best acqua vitae, and each one skein, dish, and knife before him, and when the liquor is out nail up the coffin, and commit me to the earth whence I came. This is my will; witness my hand this 3rd of March, 1674.

25. THE DAISY FIELD

There's a wealth of yellow daisies in the field beside
        my door,
    And they nod and dance before me in the sun;
Such lovely yellow daisies I have never seen before,
    And they seem to whisper, 'Come and join our
        fun!'

They are flinging back the sunlight, they are
        beautiful and gay,
    I would dearly like to join them for a while,
But of course it's quite impossible, I'm old and
        turning grey,
    And I nearly have forgotton how to smile.

And yet they sway seductively and flirting with
        the breeze,
    They would thrall me with the wanton in their
           eyes,
And I wish I were a little child to play again with
        these
    And frolic in a daisy paradise.

I wish I were a child again to mingle with their glory,
    To share the lilting laughter of the day
With sun-light and with star-shine, and Life an
        unread story,
    And all my world a daisy field in play!

26. THE LOST ONES

Somewhere is music from the linnets' bills,
And through the sunny flowers the bee-wings drone.
And white bells of convolvulus on hills
Of quiet May make silent ringing, blown
Hither and thither by the wind of showers,
And somewhere all the wandering birds have flown;
And the brown breath of Autumn chills the flowers.

But where are all the loves of long ago?
Oh, little twilight ship blown up the tide,
Where are the faces laughing in the glow
Of morning years, the lost ones scattered wide?
Give me your hand, oh brother, let us go
Crying about the dark for those who died.

27. THE REST IS SILENCE

The crowd had pressed close around the grave, their heads lowered, their faces grim and drawn. I should have been praying, but my heart and soul were numb. I looked up from the coffin and saw in the distance the face of Mary Keane. Tears were welling in her eyes. I do not know why she should, at that terrible moment in my life, remind me of a beautiful poem her husband John B Keane, the dramatist, had written for her years before, when he was going away from her for the first time:

O my love, my own love, lie down here beside me,
O my love, my dear love, O sweet love betide me,
Lie still in my arms, do not moan, love, or
    tremble,
The wild doves are sleeping high on the green
    bramble.

James continued praying:

*Show your mercy to your servant Mary who has
departed this life, that as she was numbered
among the faithful on earth she may be
brought into the company of your angels
in heaven.*

The coffin was lowered on ropes, deep down into
the grave. The words of Keane's poem still kept
haunting my mind:

*All over Feale river the shadows are falling,
And deep in Shanowen the vixen is calling,
The sweet night is young, love, the night is for
    ever,
And shadows are falling all over Feale river.*

Standing by the open grave, strange tangled
memories of the past rushed wildly through my
head. I remembered a holiday I had spent with her
in the North Kerry country at the suggestion of
John B. Arm in arm we had rambled together along
the banks of the Feale river. We watched the salmon jumping in the pools. We listened to the wild
and lonely call of the curlews returning to the
sedgy banks. We had bathed and swam in the
breaking surf at Ballybunion. In the evening we
strolled along the cliffs, watching the young lovers
beginning their lives together, as we had done so
many years before. Sometimes in the late summer
evenings we climbed the side of Knockanore
mountain. To the south we could see the vast
panorama of headlands and islands lit by the

slanting sun: Kerry Head, Mount Brandon, The Three Sisters, The Great Blasket, Inisvickallane and Inis na mBro. Across the lordly Shannon we could see her homeland, and the hills of Clare.

I would fly like a bird with white wings in the air
Or swim the wild waters far off into Clare
The sweet night is young love, the night is
*   forever,*
And shadows are falling all over Feale river.

Here my mind must have gone hysterical, for in this awful moment of pain I remembered several silly things that happened during our life; her flushing her nylon stockings down the toilet when she was tipsy; her turning the tables on a tinker who tried to sell her plate for silver; her putting the run on a Franciscan who called to the house collecting, by asking him to baby-sit for a harassed neighbour with six children, and earn the money. These, and many other utter banalities went tossing through my mind.

Then another priest, Father John O'Dwyer, said aloud the customary prayer for the mourners:

O Lord Jesus Christ, God of all consolation,
whose heart was moved to tears at the grave of
Lazarus, look now with compassion on your
servants who are sorely grieved by their loss.
Strengthen in their hearts the spirit of faith to
accept this cross from your loving hands. Give
to their troubled hearts, and to the hearts of
all men, the light of hope, that they may so live

as one day to be united again where all tears
shall be wiped away in the kingdom of your
love.

The gravediggers got ready for their grim task. A stifled sob could be heard here and there in the crowd. Somewhere in the distance the rich, triumphant voice of a lark soared upwards in lovely curves of sound through the still clear sky. Spring was back 'with rustling shade, and apple blossoms filled the air'. Mary had not failed her rendezvous.

Soon, brown earth and rock and stone would crush the frail and wasted body of the woman I loved, and would forever unite her to all that remained of the other woman closest to me in life, the woman at whose knees I learned to pray. The crowd would leave the graveyard having done their duty and paid their respects. Darkness would fall and everything would be silent and still. In a few weeks, or a few months, Mary would be forgotten by all, except by those whose bruised hearts now ached, and who would yearn for her in the long lonely nights of future years. Such is the law of life, her universal law, to be born, to live, to suffer, to die, to be forgotten. The only permanence is the permanence of change.

But there is always Hope. The hope ... *to be united again where all tears shall be wiped away in the kingdom of your love* . . . . .

28. AN POC AR BUILE

Ar mo dhul dom siar chun Droichead Uí Mhórdha,
píce im dhóid is mé ag dul i meitheal,
cé chasfaí orm i gcumar ceoidh
ach pocán crón is é ar buile.

Curfá:
Ailliliú, puilliliú, aillliú, tá an poc ar buile,
aillliú, puilliliú, aillliú, tá an poc ar buile.

Do ritheamar trasna trí ruilleogach
is do ghluais an comhrac ar fud na muinge,
is treascairt dá bhfuair sé sna turtóga,
chuas ina ainneoin ar a dhroim le fuinneamh.

Curfá

Níor fhág sé carraig go raibh scót ann
ná gur rith le fórsa chun mé a mhilleadh,
is ea ansan do chaith sé an léim ba mhó
le fána mór na Faille Brice.

Curfá

Bhí garda mór i mBaile an Róistigh
is bhailigh fórsaí chun sinn a chlipeadh,
do bhuail sé rop dá adhairc sa tóin air
is dá bhrístí nua do dhein sé giobail.

Curfá

29. THE END

'...The law under which I suffer is surely a severe one — may the makers and promoters of it be justified in the integrity of their motives, and the purity of their own lives! By that law I am stamped a felon, but my heart disdains the imputation.

My comfortable lot, and industrious course of life, best refute the charge of being an adventurer for plunder; but if to have loved my country — to have known its wrongs — to have felt the injuries of the persecuted Catholics, and to have united with them and all other religious persuasions in the most orderly and least sanguinary means of procuring redress — if those be felonies, I am a felon, but not otherwise...

To the generous protection of my country I leave a beloved wife, who has been constant and true to me, and whose grief for my fate has already nearly occasioned her death. I have five living children, who have been my delight. May they love their country as I have done, and die for it if needful...

I trust that all my virtuous countrymen will bear me in their kind remembrance, and continue true and faithful to each other as I have been to all of them. With this last wish of my heart — nothing doubting of the success of that cause for which I suffer, and hoping for God's merciful forgiveness of such offences as my frail nature may have at any

time betrayed me into — I die in peace and charity
with all mankind.'

30. LITTLE BALL OF YARN

In the merry month of June
When the roses were in bloom
And the little birds were singing their sweet charms
Sure I spied a pretty Miss
And I kindly asked her this
'May I wind up your little ball of yarn?'

'Yerra no, kind sir,' said she
'You're a stranger unto me
And perhaps you've got some dearly other charmer.'
'Yerra no, my turtle dove
You're the only one I love
And won't meddle with your little ball of yarn.'

Now I took her to a grove
Beneath a shady green
With no intentions of doing her any harm
And to my great surprise
When I looked into her eyes
I was winding up her little ball of yarn.

Now nine months have passed and gone
Since I met this fair young one
And now she's holding a baby in her arm

I said, 'my pretty Miss
Sure I never dreamed of this
When I was winding up your little ball of yarn'.

Now come all ye young and old
Take a warning when you're told
Never rise too early in the morn
Be like the blackbird and the thrush,
Keep one hand upon your bush
And the other on your little ball of yarn.

31. CAVEAT EMPTOR

Crimes and misdemeanours against a person's sexual well-being and rights are treated of in the Brehon laws. We can get a glimpse of the type of society for which these laws were framed by noting some of the matters mentioned throughout the various tracts.

While there is no mention anywhere of barbaric crimes, such as the excision of the clitoris or the removal of female breasts, there is a rather interesting article on the penalties for castration. Each possible eventuality is foreseen in the tract:
1) If a man's penis is cut off, the wretched sufferer is entitled to two kinds of compensation for his loss. Naturally, his full honour-price had to be paid and in addition to this the atonement called *corp-díre* in full. The term used for 'penis' in

this tract is *uidim* and it should be noted that it is a word which could also mean 'implement, instrument or tool.'

11) The case of him whose scrotum is cut off comes next. For some odd reason only full *corp-dire* is payable in this case. One wonders how the victim's honour is unaffected in such a situation. Perhaps this was rare and even unknown. In many places in the Brehon law tracts the legislators set out examples which were merely notional and dredged up from their inventive lawyers' minds.

111) The tract then discusses the fellow whose left testicle only is removed. For this deed the penalty was full body-price or *corp-dire*. The reason for this has its roots in medical theory. It was thought that the left testicle was the active agent in procreation and they evidently regarded the companion as a balancing ornament.

(IV) As might be anticipated the removal of the right testicle earned a penalty which was equal to part of the body-price. A man's fertility, the lawyers reasoned, was not seriously affected by this act.

(V) The final detail is that a much diminished penalty for full castration is payable to a man in Holy Orders or a decrepit old fellow. Reasonably enough it is stated that such a person had no need of his generative organs. For the removal of his excess organs the castrator was penalised according to the severity of the wound inflicted on his victim, as he would be in the case of wounding any other part of the body.

The Brehon laws distinguished between two types of rape. One was the violent possession of a woman sexually and the other was to make love to her by deceit when she was asleep and could not give her consent.

In the old stories, which may be historical or at least based on what happened in the earliest times, there is a story of rape which is worth retelling. We hear that Ailill Olum, Bare-eared Ailill, earned his sobriquet in the following manner. Ailill defeated and slew a rival king in battle. He then laid hands on the dead man's daughter and proceeded to rape her. This spirited young lady resisted him so violently that she bit off his two ears and earned him his unusual nickname. Ailill was so infuriated by her assault on his person that he transfixed her with his spear to the ground and killed her instantly. The point of his spear struck a stone underneath her and was bent. He attempted to straighten the spear-point with his teeth but this blackened his teeth and his breath became foul henceforth. It is tempting to see all this as an allegory. The old story relates that Ailill was bound by *gessa* or taboos not to bend the point of his spear on a stone; not to kill a woman with his spear; not to straighten his spear-point with his teeth. All these he had violated. It is difficult not to see the spear as a phallic symbol, the stone as an unwilling woman, and his slaying of her as his attempted rape. What the significance of the fouling of his breath and the blackening of his teeth may be, can be left to the vaulting imagination of the individual reader.

32. YOUNG LOVE

Beidh aonach amárach i gContae an Chláir (fá thrí)
cén mhaith dom é, ní bheidh mé ann?

Curfá:

A mháithrín, an ligfidh tú chun aonaigh mé? (fá thrí)
a mhuirnín ó, ná héiligh é.

Níl tú a deich nó a haon déag fós (fá thrí)
nuair a bheidh tú trí déag beidh tú mór.

Curfá

B'fhearr liom féin mo ghréasaí bróg (fá thrí)
ná oifigeach airm faoi lásaí óir.

Curfá

33. BOYHOOD

Always as a small boy I had a great longing to go to
the mountains, particularly on sunny mornings
when the air was fragrant and skies were blue. One
could see the mountains at play-time from the
back of the school. They stood independent,
unchanging and mysterious. They were odd fel-

lows, the mountains – odder than my Uncle Dan, who was an odd as two right boots. When summer hazes tinted their blue outlines they looked unbelievably beautiful and it was hard on a small boy to whom a classroom was prison.

I pestered my parents to let me go and stay with my faraway relatives and eventually they entered into correspondence with them, who, since they had no way of knowing about me, were eager to accept me. My paternal grandmother was a mountainy woman, and that was excuse enough.

At length, as the schoolteachers say, I reached the manly age of eight and the school closed for the summer holidays. When the time came to go to the mountain, I refused, but complaints were arriving at home daily about such heinous offences as robbing orchards and tying pieces of thread to door-knockers. I got a lift from a local Creamery lorry and, with my brown suitcase between my legs, set off into the unknown.

For the next five years I never missed the summer holidays in the Stacks' Mountains. Those were wonderful days and it was there, for the first time, that I met characters who mattered and people who left a real impression. These were lively and vital people, composed of infinite merriment and a little sadness. They lived according to their means and if you didn't like them you could leave them. When they went into town they drank and were misunderstood. Their liveliness and strength was misinterpreted. Rows took place and the age-old hatred of country for town was resurrected. It still exists. It was in the Stacks' Mountains that I discovered that the Holy Ghost was born in

Lyreacrompane.

'Some people claim 'twas Glin,' an old man informed me, pointing at a mountain, 'and more says 'tis Clonakilty, but 'tis up there He was born.'

There were several matchmakers in the locality then; six people who had been accused of evil-eye work, and twenty of the most inventive, astonishing and likeable liars on the face of creation.

It is here I learned the great ballad: *The Road to Athea*, which contains the classic stanza:

> *We arrived in Athea at a quarter to one*
> *And up to the clergy we quickly did run;*
> *'Twas there we were married without*
> *   much delay;*
> *And we broke a spring bed that night in*
> *   Athea.*

34. LOVE LETTERS

A fragrant perfume clings around them still,
    Of violets, and clover, and of thyme,
And memories of one fair woodland hill,
    And You and I where rambling roses climb.

Of You and I, the dear, dear dreams we planned —
    The vows we gave, and whispered soft and low —
The centuries our deathless love had spanned —
    And that was only one short year ago.

'Forever thine'. 'Thine own till life is run,'
    Your letters read. My head swims fast awhirl —
For you are married to another one,
    And I, tomorrow, wed another girl.

35. SHANNON INTERLUDE

It is the little unplanned interludes like this I find
so charming about cruising on the Shannon. You
quickly come to terms with the inevitable fact that
hurry and bustle will get you nowhere, and as you
do, all tension and anxiety seem to vanish as an
untroubled and mysterious peace casts a spell over
your soul. Meelick, almost inaccessible by road, is
one of the Shannon's secret places; a place where
time stands still and where a weary human spirit
can soar above a world of blighted hopes. Having
strolled along overgrown pathways for nearly half-
an-hour I found a pleasant resting place under a
wild hawthorn bush just beginning to drop its
blossoms one by one. Maxie lay at my feet,
surrounded by a carpet of golden buttercups, still
panting after his forays and feats in the world
beneath the bushes and trees. In the distance I
could hear the soft soothing sound of the murmur-
ing water falling over the salmon weir, like the
sound of music lost somewhere in space and
contrasting strangely with the little whispering
noises that came from the grass and the buzzing of

the insects like telegraph wires in a summer's breeze. Everywhere around me birds were singing joyously; blackbird, thrush, goldfinch, starling and many others — Meelick was one of the few places on the Shannon where I heard such a melody of wild song. The whole atmosphere was permeated with the sad loveliness of life. Overheard, a lark, suspended high in the sky dropped golden chords of exquisite music on to the rolling meadows. I envied that lark who had something we humans hadn't, two worlds to live in — the blue sky and the rich earth, and then the words of that most beautiful of Irish songs *The Lark in the Clear Air* tumbled through my head:

Dear thoughts are in my mind
And my soul soars enchanted
As I hear the sweet lark sing
In the clear air of the day
For a tender beaming smile
To my hope has been granted
And tomorrow she shall hear
All my fond heart would say.

'The world is a study that did not quite come off,' moaned Van Gogh. I do not agree. We live in a marvellous world but many of us seem to be in too much of a hurry ever to become aware of it. Very often, however, in the quiet moments of a holiday, we get a tiny glimpse of what we are missing, and the beauty all around us stirs up strange vague feelings that are very hard to define, but which give us the sense of a deep incompleteness in our lives. Yet I think if we just pause awhile and not be frightened by this feeling and listen carefully we will hear, not only the music from outside, but an inner music of the soul which harmonises with it, and it will then seem that there is no real division between ourselves and the beauty of the universe. The infinite cannot be divided against itself. Even though man is an insignificant speck he is still part of a God's dream which has no end. 'In a rest which is meditative and attentive,' said Amiel, 'the wrinkles of the soul are smoothed away, and the soul itself spreads, unfolds and springs afresh, and like the trodden grass of the roadside, or the bruised leaf of a plant, repairs its injuries, becomes new, spontaneous, true and original.' There is always a little left from what floats in the wake of our dreams.

36. BLIND LOVE

Oh, dark, sweetest girl, are my days doomed to be,
While my heart bleeds in silence and sorrow for thee:
In the green spring of life to the grave I go down,
Oh! shield me, and save me, my lov'd Peggy Browne.

I dreamt that at evening my footsteps were bound
To yon deep spreading wood where the shades fall
    around.
I sought, midst new scenes, all my sorrows to drown,
But the cure of my grief rests with thee, Peggy
    Browne.

'Tis soothing, sweet maiden, thy accents to hear,
For, like wild fairy music they melt on the ear,
Thy breast is as fair as the swans clothed in down,
Oh, peerless and perfect's my own Peggy Browne.

Dear, dear is the bark to its own cherished tree,
But dearer, far dearer, is my lov'd one to me:
In my dreams I draw near her, uncheck'd by a frown,
But my arms spread in vain to embrace Peggy
　　　Browne.

37. LAST POEM

I do not grudge them; Lord, I do not grudge
My two strong sons that I have seen go out
To break their strength and die, they and a few,
In bloody protest for a glorious thing.
They shall be spoken of among their people,
The generations shall remember them,
And call them blessed;
But I will speak their names to my own heart
In the long nights;
The little names that were familiar once
Round my dead hearth.
Lord, thou art hard on mothers:
We suffer in their coming and their going;
And tho' I grudge them not, I weary, weary
Of the long sorrow — And yet I have my joy:
My sons were faithful, and they fought.

38. THE WAKE

The bishop, Most Rev. Dr. William Higgins, announced the following regulations regarding wakes:

'We are saddened and heartbroken to learn that much evil is resulting from rough wakes among our people, and that the behaviour of young people is being affected by them. We, therefore, request the clergy to endeavour to eradicate such abuses in their own parishes. They must point out to the parishioners that the playing of lewd games at wakes, where Death should rather be pondered on, is synonymous with turning their backs on their Faith. The clergy must take care to ensure that indecent talk and especially the sinful practice of travestying the Sacrament of Marriage are abolished on such occasions. Parish priests are to ensure that prayers are recited for the soul of the deceased and that spiritual books are read. Unmarried young men and women are solemnly forbidden to attend wakes between sunset and sunrise, with the exception of those who are related by blood or by marriage with the deceased.'

39. THE MOON BEHIND THE HILL

I watched last night the rising moon
Upon a foreign strand,
Till memories came like flowers of June,
Of home and fatherland;
I dreamt I was a child once more
Beside the rippling rill,
Where first I saw in days of yore
The moon behind the hill.

It brought me back the visions grand
That purpled boyhood's dreams;
Its youthful loves, its happy land,
As bright as mornings beams.
It brought me back my own sweet Nore,
The castle and the mill,
Until my eyes could see no more
The moon behind the hill.

It brought me back a mother's love
Until, in accents wild,
I prayed her from her home above
To guard her lonely child;
It brought me once across the wave,
To live in memory still –
It brought me back my Kathleen's grave
The moon behind the hill.

40. IRISH POET

He is a poet on two levels; he is both a concrete and an abstract poet. Every abstract poem he writes is important but obscure. It might be said that the more obscure the meaning the better the poem. Several of these poems have been published in the little magazines, a fact of which he is justifiably proud. This little abstract poem of his illustrates, I think, the depth and intensity of his feelings. Since its meaning is not immediately clear it is obviously an important work. I will allow you to judge for yourself. Here it is.

> *The blood-beaked bird*
> *On the elm*
> *Smells strangers,*
> *Leaving the hare*
> *Trembling above the*
> *Down beat of*
> *The curlew's wing.*

He has also tried his hand at what is called diamond poetry. One example must suffice here, a pleasant little nugget entitled *Duality*, visually like a candlestick or a slender vase, graceful and shapely, but possibly a little unsteady at its base:

DUALITY

I
d o
n o t
S e e m
E q u a l
W h i l e
I
a m
i n
o n e
o r
t w o
P i e c e s

41. GETHSEMANE

Breathes there a man who claimeth not
One lonely spot,
    His own Gethsemane,
Whither with his inmost pain
He fain
    Would weary plod,
Find the surcease that is known
In wind a-moan
    And sobbing sea,
Cry his sorrow hid of men
And then —
    Touch hands with God.

42. POLITENESS

Now, Father MacGillacuddy's parish clerk was a tall graceful man falling slightly into flesh, with a soft serene countenance like you'd see on a tom cat after drinking a lot of milk. He was slow and stately in his gait as he walked the road, a straight back on him, you'd swear he'd swallowed a crowbar, and a long black coat buttoned up to the chin. Ideas above his station! You could forgive passing strangers for tipping the hat to him. Only for he keeping out of the bishop's way people said he'd have got a parish, for he was very devout.

When the bishop was coming for confirmation, Father Mac put the parish clerk whitewashing the dry wall in front of the house. The parish clerk got his bucket and set into work making short lazy brush strokes in time with the slow air of a hymn — you'd know by him that he'd love to give out benediction!

> *Hail Queen of Heaven the Ocean star,*
> *Guide of the wanderer here below,*
> *Thrown on life's surge, we implore,*
> *Save us from peril and from woe!*

Along came Father Mac. 'Very nice,' he said, 'singing at your work and a hymn too. Very laudable, but show me the brush. Don't you think this would be more suitable,' he said as he changed the tempo to:

64

Father O'Flynn you've a wonderful way
*   with you,*
All the old ladies are longing to pray with
*   you,*
All the young women are longing to play
*   with you,*
You have a way with you Father O'Flynn!

The bishop was very old and didn't even notice the whitewash when he came. The confirmation was held that year in the outside chapel, five miles away from the presbytery, and the bishop, because of his age, was short-taken during the ceremony, and the parish clerk brought him out the sacristy door and ducked into Hannah Maroya's. She had a contraption in the yard, the missioners used to stay there. Hannah Maroya's man that made it. He threw his hat down on the bottom of a tay chest, drew the pencil around it, cut out the hole and propped the chest over the stream in the back garden. But Hannah Maroya thought that a bit draughty for a bishop, so she said, 'Wait a minute my Lord.'

She wasn't long away, but the bishop thought it was an eternity.

'This way your Lordship,' she said and she took him down in the parlour and there, with a good sup of hot water at the bottom to knock the sting out of it, was a big chainaware pot and a blessed candle lighting at each side of it! That was respect!

43. PROBLEM

I won't marry a man that is rich,
For he'd do nothing but sit in a ditch;
I won't marry at all, at all;
I won't marry at all.

I won't marry a man that is poor,
For he'd go begging from door to door;
I won't marry at all, at all;
I won't marry at all.

I won't marry a man that is old,
For he'd do nothing but fight and scold;
I won't marry at all, at all;
I won't marry at all.

I won't marry a man that is young,
For he'd do nothing but look for fun;
I won't marry at all, at all;
I won't marry at all.

So I'll take my stool and sit in the shade,
For I'm determined to die an old maid;
I won't marry at all, at all;
I won't marry at all.

44. LOYALTY

We, your Majesty's subjects, the Roman Catholic Clergy of the Kingdom of Ireland together assembled, do hereby declare and solemnly protest, before God and his holy angels, that we own and acknowledge your Majesty to be our true and lawful King, supreme Lord, and undoubted Sovereign, as well of this realm of Ireland as of all other your Majesty's dominions; consequently we confess ourselves bound in conscience to be obedient to your Majesty in all civil and temporal affairs, as any subject ought to be to his prince, and as the laws of God and nature require at our hands. Therefore we promise that we will inviolably bear true allegiance to your Majesty, your lawful heirs and successors; and that no power on earth shall be able to withdraw us from our duty herein: and that we will, even to the loss of our blood, if occasion requires, assert your Majesty's rights against any that shall invade the same, or attempt to deprive yourself, or your lawful heirs and successors, of any part thereof. And to the end this our sincere protestation may more clearly appear, we further declare, that it is not our doctrine, that subjects may be discharged, absolved, or freed from the obligation of performing their duty of true obedience and allegiance to their prince: much less may we allow of, or pass as tolerable, any doctrine that perniciously, or against the word of God, maintains, that any private subject may lawfully kill or murder the anointed of God, his prince. Wherefore, pursuant to the deep apprehension we have of the abomination and sad consequences of its practice, we do engage ourselves to discover to your Majesty, or some of your ministers, any attempt of that kind, rebellion or conspiracy, against your Majesty's person, crown, or royal authority, that comes to our knowledge, whereby such horrid evil may be prevented. Finally, as we hold the premises to be agreeable to good conscience, so we religiously swear the due observance thereof to our utmost; and we will preach and teach the same to our respective flocks. In witness whereof we do hereunto subscribe the day of June, 1666.

45. LIGHT HEART

There is Springtime in the Heavens, and there's
        Springtime in the breeze,
And the birds are singing Spring songs in the
        blossom-laden trees;
The days are growing longer, and there's warmth
        in the air,
And there's sweetness just in living, and there's
        gladness everywhere;
      And, yet you say you're lonely, Lad,
      Lonely, why?
Isn't the shimmering, shining sun smiling in the
        sky?
Isn't it smiling at you in a friendly kind of way,
Doesn't it look as if it wished to bid you time o'
        day?

Lonely, why, Lord love you,
   You're just blue!
Lonely, when each living thing wants to be your
         friend,
   And God is in his Heaven;
Lonely when there's love for you and kindness
         without end!
   Lonely, you're not lonely, Lad,
   A little blue, a little sad.
Come, cheer up, Laddie; cheer up, Son,
There's lots of pleasure, lots of fun,
Left in the world for every one.

There is Winter in the Heavens, and there's Winter
         in the wind,
There is Winter in the tree-tops, but, is Winter so
         unkind?
The days are growing shorter, and the nights are
         long and cold,
But, the stars they shine much brighter, and they
         wink and twinkle gold;
   And you again are lonely, Lad,
   Lonely, why?
Isn't every snow-flake in the sullen, silent sky
A little pearly tear-drop from an angel, come to
         bless,
To lay itself against your cheek in gentle, soft
         caress?
   Lonely, why, God bless you,
   You're just blue!
Lonely, when the crackling frost brings gladness to
         the ear,
   And God is in his Heaven;

69

Lonely, when about you you can feel King Winter
            near;
      Lonely, you're not lonely, Lad,
      A little blue, a little sad.
Go, dry your tears, be happy, Son,
There's lots of pleasure, lots of fun,
Left in the world for every one!

46. HOPE

Where are the best quality cattle to be found? A
correspondent says in County Clare. Ennis, he
states is about the best centre and crafty farmers
from all parts come to Ennis for stock bulls. I have
seen them to breed better than themselves. In time
to come every large farmer will learn the secret.

47. A REQUEST

Give me but six foot three (one inch to spare)
Of Irish ground, and dig it anywhere;
And for my poor soul say an Irish prayer
            Above the spot.

Let it be where cloud and mountain meet,
Or vale where grows the tufted meadow-sweet,
Or boreen trod by peasants' shoeless feet;
            It matters not.

I loved them all, the vale, the hill,
The moaning sea, the water-lilied rill,
The yellow furze, the lake shore lone and still,
            The wild bird's song.

But more than hill or valley, bird or moor,
More than the green fields of my native Suir,
I loved those hapless ones, the Irish poor,
            All my life long.

Little I did for them in outward deed,
And yet be unto them of praise the meed
For the stiff fight I waged 'gainst lust and greed
            I learnt it there.

So give me Irish grave, mid Irish air,
With Irish grass above it anywhere;
And let some passing peasant give a prayer
            For a soul there.

48. RECORDS

It is said that Ireland was first inhabited by Final Palaeolithic Hunters around 9,000 B.C. Some of their physical attributes and feats of endurance are worth noting.

Tallest Irishman: Although Jim Cully, Tipperary is, at 7 feet 2 inches, the best-known tall man, Patrick Cotter O'Brien of Kinsale, Co. Cork is said to have measured 8 feet 7¾ inches. Porthumous calculations, however, put his height at 7 feet 10.86 inches.

Smallest Irishman: David Jones, Lisburn, Co. Antrim, born 28 April 1903, measured an unconfirmed 2 feet 2 inches at death on 28 March 1970. His weight of 4 stone, however, suggests a height of approximately 3 feet.

Smallest Irishwoman: Catherine Kelly who died at Norwich, England in October 1785 was recorded as being 34 inches in height. Weighing 1 stone 8 pounds she was nicknamed 'The Irish Fairy'.

Heaviest Irishman: Roger Byrne, Rosenallis, Co. Laois who died in 1808 weighed 52 stone.

Oldest Man: In 1887, James Warren, Baldoyle, Co. Dublin died at the age of 167.

Oldest Woman: When the Countess of Desmond fell from her cherry tree and was killed in 1604 she was aged 140 years.

Oldest Mother: Mrs Mary Higgins, Cork City, who was born on 7 January 1876, gave birth to a baby girl on St Patrick's Day 1931 when aged 55 years and 69 days.

Oldest Father: There is a record of an unnamed man becoming a father at 89 years.

Tallest Corpse: The preserved body of an 8 foot tall Crusader may be seen at St Michan's Vaults, Dublin where, due to unique atmospheric conditions, bodies do not decompose.

Quiet Baby: The first baby born in Ireland using the 'Birth Without Violence' technique (the Leboyer Method) was Zaharra Grace, daughter of Anthony and Naja O'Brien, in December 1976.

Oldest Triplets: Still alive in 1978, Anthony, Joseph and Edmund McMahon were born in Coore East, Co. Clare in 1898.

Old Folks' County: Highest proportion of geriatrics in any county is Donegal with 16% of its population.

Longest and Deepest Underwater: When they sank 1,757 feet about 150 miles off the Cork coast on 29 August 1973, Roger C. Chapman and Roger Mallinson were trapped for 76 hours.

Longest Hunger Strike: 94 days, a world record, at Cork Jail from 11 August to 12 November 1920. Nine of the twelve strikers survived: Sean Hennessy, John Crowley, Christopher Upton, Peter Crowley, John Power, Joseph Kelly, Michael Burke, Michael O'Reilly and Thomas Donovan.

Longest Kidnap: Dr Herrema, Dutch Industrialist, Kidnapped at Limerick on 3 October 1975 and held for 36 days which included an 18 day siege in a house at St Evan's Park, Monasterevin, Co. Kildare.

Shot Before Birth: Catherine Anne Gilmore was delivered by Caesarean section three months prematurely in July 1976. Her mother had been shot in the Ardoyne district of Belfast and a bullet had lodged in her baby's back. It was removed and the child released from hospital eight months later.

Long Skip: On 25 June 1977 a Waterford boxer, Paddy 'Flutter' Reilly, kept up a non-stop skipping routine for 5 hours, 41 minutes to make an Irish and world record.

Oyster Opening: Willie Moran, The Weir, Kilcolgan, Co. Galway, opened a record 30 oysters in 1 minute 31 seconds at Clarenbridge, Co. Galway on 10 September 1977.

Strong Man: The late Michael 'Butty' Sugrue from Killorglin, Co. Kerry was Ireland's strongest man. Among his feats of strength was the pulling of a passenger-laden double decker bus.

Gulp and Croak: John McNamara, Scariff, Co. Clare won the first frog-swallowing championship of Ireland at Ballycumber, Co. Offaly in 1975 swallowing five live frogs in 1 minute 5 seconds.

U.S. Crossing: Tom McGrath, Eddery, Co. Fermanagh, ran 3,046 miles from New York to San Francisco in September-October 1977. His record time of 53 days 7 minutes was made during his honeymoon.

Live Burial: Tim Hayes, Cobh, Co. Cork remained buried alive for 215 hours in an 8 foot grave at Newbridge, Co. Derry between 4 and 18 July 1967. His coffin was 6 feet 3 inches long, 12 inches wide at head and feet, 21 inches wide at shoulders and 14 inches deep.

Never Trailing: 32 members of Dublin Fire Brigade hauled a trailer and pump from Dublin's Mansion House to Cork's City Hall in 21 hours to set up a world record on 30-31 March, 1978.

49. RETURNED PICTURE

Refused admission! Baby, Baby,
Don't you feel a little pain.
See, your picture with your mother's
From the prison back again.
They are cruel, cruel jailers —
They are heartless, heartless men.

Was it much to ask them Baby —
These rough menials of the Queen —
Was it much to ask to give him
This poor picture form and mien
Of the wife he loved, the little son
He never yet had seen?

Ah you laugh, my little Flax-Hair!
But my eyes are full of tears;
And my heart is sorely troubled
With old voices in my ears;
With the lingering disappointment
That is shadowing my years!

50. AVE ET VALE

The scum and the dregs of this wretched country
are now in power. I don't know where my old dear
Ireland has gone.

51. MORAL FORCE

But war must be faced and blood must be shed, not gleefully, but as a terrible necessity, because there are moral horrors worse than any physical horror, because freedom is indispensable for a soul erect, and freedom must be had at any cost of suffering; the soul is greater than the body. This is the justification of war. If hesitating to undertake it means the overthrow of liberty possessed, or the lying passive in slavery already accomplished, then it is the duty of every man to fight if he is standing, or revolt if he is down. And he must make no peace till freedom is assured, for the moral plague that eats up a people whose independence is lost is more calamitous than any physical rending of limb from limb. The body is a passing phase; the spirit is immortal; and the degradation of that immortal part of man is the great tragedy of life. Consider all the mean things and debasing tendencies that wither up a people in a state of slavery. There are the bribes of those in power to maintain their ascendancy, the barter of every principle by time-servers; the corruption of public life and the apathy of private life; the hard struggle of those of high ideals, the conflict with all ignoble practices, the wearing down of patience, and in the end the quiet abandoning of the flag once bravely flourish-ed; then the increased numbers of the apathetic and the general gloom, depression, and despair — everywhere a land decaying. Viciousness, mean-ness, cowardice, intolerance, every bad thing arises like a weed in the night and blights the land where freedom is dead; and the aspect of that land and the soul of that people become spectacles of disgust, revolting and terrible, terrible for the high things degraded and the great destinies imperilled. It would be less terrible if an earthquake split the land in two, and sank it into the ocean. To avert the moral plague of slavery men fly to arms, notwithstanding the physical consequence, and those who set more count by the physical consequences cannot by that avert them, for the moral disease is followed by physical wreck—if delayed still inevitable. So, physical force is justified, not *per se*, but as an expression of moral force; where it is unsupported by the higher principle it is evil incarnate. The true antithesis is not between moral force and physical force, but between moral force and moral weakness. That is the fundamental distinction being ignored on all sides. When the time demands and the occasion offers, it is imperative to have recourse to arms, but in that terrible crisis we must preserve our balance. If we leap forward for our enemies' blood, glorifying brute force, we set up the standard of the tyrant and heap up infamy for ourselves; on the other hand, if we hesitate to take the stern action demanded, we fail in strength of soul, and let slip the dogs of war to every extreme of weakness and wildness, to create depravity and horror that will ultimately destroy us. A true soldier of freedom will not hesitate to strike vigorously and strike home, knowing that on his resolution will depend the restoration and defence of liberty.

52. MY LIPS WOULD SING

My lips would sing a song for you, a soulful little
        song for you,
    A plaintive little song for you, upon a summer's
        day;
But for the very life of me, the merry, merry life of
        me,
    The laughter-loving life of me, I cannot but be
        gay.

For oh, the sun is shining, Dear, and who could be
        repining, Dear,
    And who would be unhappy, Dear, when all
        the world is young?
So I will hum a melody, a mirthful little melody,
    A joyous little melody that never yet was sung.

And you shall hear of Fairyland, of Kings and
        Queens of Fairyland,
    Of men and maids of Fairyland, and Love shall
        be the theme,
And straight before your brimming eyes, a golden
        glint of Paradise
    Shall steal, My Dear, to still your sighs, and
        give you back your dream.

And you will taste of happiness, a tiny bit of
        happiness,
    A wistful bit of happiness, upon a summer's
        day;
And just a little smile from you, a sunny little smile
        from you,
    A trembly little smile from you shall be a poet's
        pay.

53. GREAT LIES

'Did I ever tell you,' said Lahy, 'about the day I was fishing in the Lakes of Killarney? Well, the fish were very scarce, but about three o'clock in the evening I hooked this big salmon and he jumped and thrashed and tore around the lake and me after him on the bank. Well, after an hour and a half he was dead bate and I hauled him in on the shore. There was a crowd gathered and they all said that he was the biggest salmon ever caught in Kerry. Well, it took six strong men to carry him a hundred yards to the nearest pub.

'We were inside having drinks and we didn't feel the time passing when this man, with specs and a bowler hat, came in.

"Which of ye caught the salmon?" he said.

"I did," says I.

"Well, you'll have to put him back in the lake again," says he. "I'm the County Engineer!'

"Why for?" says I.

"The level of the lake is after falling two feet," he says, "and you'll get six months in jail for that."

'I declare to me God hadn't the six men to carry him back and put him in the water, and the level of the lake rose again. You see, the fellow with the bowler hat told me afterwards over a drink that the whole trouble was, that the people of Killarney kicked up murder on account of there bein' no water to flush their privys and the stink from all the houses was something shocking!'

****

'There was an educated man telling me,' said Dan the Rat, 'that our family could be traced back to an Irish King, a fellow be the name of Brian Boru. We're descended from him — and that man knew what he was talking about.'

'Well, the schoolmaster told me,' said Thady the Turnip, 'that our family could be traced back to Noah. One of them was in the Ark with him.'

'Well, me mother, God rest her,' said Lahy, 'always told me that the ould people told her that at the time of the Flood our family had their own boat!'

****

'I remember one time,' said Phil the Fool, 'we was driving cattle over the Knockmeldown mountains and we came to a lake of water called "Petticoatloose". Well, if you stood beside the lake and shouted, "Up De Valera", the sound of your words would come back three times to you. An echo, or something like that, the other lads called it.'

'That's right,' said Lahy. 'That could happen. I was working for a farmer between Cahir and Mitchelstown and there was a big cave there and every night before I went to bed I'd go to the mouth of the cave and shout; "Wake up Lahy," and the echo would wake me at six o'clock in the morning in time for the early milking!'

54. COLONEL BLIMP

These are the people you want to put over the Dutch in South Africa. You want a settlement. You want the two races to mingle hand in hand waving the Union Jack and singing *Rule Britannia* and you would put in ascendency over the Dutch such men as have made their ascendency in Ireland hateful. I understand the principles of Pirate Smith who hoisted his black flag at Bristol and made war with all and sundry for the sake of booty. He had not a Bible on board. He swore by the Jolly Roger and not by the Ten Commandments. You want to syndicate Christianity, and take the Twelve Apostles into your limited liability company. Then you hold up your hands like the pharisee and invite other nations to rejoice that the English possess such virtues. The Irish people are a feeble folk and the only advantage which the Irish have is that we are able to contemplate your virtues at close quarters... Your policy is a policy of grab, and I do think it is pitiable that a nation whose qualities are great, whose courage is indomitable, whose resources are endless, should have, at this day, the canker of corruption eating at her heart. The principles which made you great are forgotten. The principles which made the British name a terror are represented by a statue of Cromwell outside Westminster Hall. We represent a small country, but we have memories and we have hopes and here lift up the voice of that country in protest against your policy and we declare that the men of Ireland will never join you in any composition of wrong or of injustice.

55. SLÁN

Ó, a Dhaid bhoicht, tá na comharsain go léir ag
teacht ag crothadh lámh leat inniu fé rachaidh tú sa
chónra. Ní bhfaighidh tú fáilte a chur roimh aon
cheann acu anois, is ba é tusa an fear bocht a
mbeadh a chathaoir is a stól i gcóir aige do gach
aon triúntaí bocht a thiocfadh isteach, is amasa an
lá a phós tú mo mháthair ní raibh mórán córacha
agat chun éinne a chur in shuí iontu. Ní raibh tada
agat féin is ag mo mháthair a shuífeá air an chéad lá
ach an dá chloch ghorm a thug tú isteach ón chnoc,
is bhíodh an saol is a mháthair ag gáirí fút a d'iarraidh mionnán an ghabhair d'fhriotháladh ar thae
dubh, is thóg tú í is gabhair ba ea í chomh rathúil is
a tógadh ag bun sléibhe riamh. Nuair a bhí sí tógtha
agat cheannaigh tú lao baineann is thóg sí duit í
agus chuir sí strus ar an gcnoc. Bhain tú cré bhuí
ina tonnaí, thóg tú fallaí is tithe, thugais scoil is
léann domsa is do mo dheifiúracha agus chuiris thar
na farraigí sinn ag múineadh do na huaisle amuigh
an teanga bheag Gaeilge a d'oil tú féin dúinn cois
na tine beag móna an oíche gheimhridh is b'shin an
tine bheag lách mhacánta nár cuireadh mias de
mhin bhuí le héinne eile sa chorcán ann riamh. Má
chaill tusa cnaipe do léine féin chuiris greim inti tú
féin fé n-iarrfá tamall do sprong ar éinne chun an
bothán a ghlanadh. Ní fhaca éinne beo tú féin is do
chomharsain ag dlí ná bínse riamh, agus má dhó-
fadh luaith an tinteáin aon chúinne den ghairdín is
tusa an fear a bhí inniúil ar an tobar a iompó air go
canta. Is tá a shliocht ort. D'éirigh leat. Níor
tháinig báille ná píléir riamh go dtí do dhoras ná

muilleoir ná fear ná bean d'aon chasóg níor dhorchaíodar do thairseach riamh ar lorg a gcoda. Tháinig tú ar na spainnéirí beaga a chuir tú ar na cnoic, is níor chaill tú ribe gruaige de d'cheann leo. Agus is tusa a shásaigh an máistir is a ghlan a shrón go calma le ciarsúir bheag do phóca ag cur an uisce ag rith ar an mbóthar díreach ar an gcnoc. Chuiris airgead geal is airgead rua i gcomhad sa bhanc dúinn, is bhris tú is shaothraigh tú an áit a raibh an stolla ábhalmhór ar an gcnoc a chuireadh eagla ar aon fhear nó bean a ghaibh thairis riamh, agus d'fhágais go brothallach i do dhiaidh anois againn an pionta bainne beirithe is an builín briste thíos ann. D'fhágais peidhre capall i do dhiaidh, is go deimhin is go diailim ní bhfaigheadh Tadhg Peidléir ná a bhean a rá gur capaill gan cruite iad! Agus anois, a Dhaid bhoicht, tógfaimidne an bóthar ceanann céanna díreach a thóg tusa, mar is é an bóthar díreach an bóthar gairid i ndeireadh na scríbe agus is mó duine a chuir a cheann ar chruach is dreodh air ina dhiaidh é, ach aon rud a leag tusa do lámh air riamh bhí ádh leis is níor imigh do chuid sochair go léir i mbláthach riamh. Ach anois, a Dhaid bhoicht, caithfidh mé do chónra d'fháil is tú a shocrú isteach inti go snasta is ní fheicfimid a chéile go deo arís go dtí Bruinne an Bhrátha, ach má fhéadfaidh tú a chuige é tar ár bhféachaint Oíche na Marbh beidh tine mhaith mhóna socruithe síos agamsa duit is do phíopa lán i bpoillín an iarta. Dia leat anois, a Dhaid bhoicht, is chím na haingil ag soilsiú ort go brothallach, is tá amhras agam go bhfuil Dia buíoch diot. Ó nár ghearr tú srón aon pháiste ar an saol seo, ní chaithfear aon íle ar t-aibíd sa saol eile.

83

56. DESTINY

Now welcome, welcome, baby-boy, unto a mother's
    fears,
The pleasure of her sufferings, the rainbow of her
    tears,
The object of your father's hope, in all he hopes to
    do,
A future man of his own land, to live him o'er anew!

How fondly on thy little brow a mother's eye would
    trace,
And in thy little limbs, and in each feature of thy
    face,
His beauty, worth, and manliness, and everything
    that's his,
Except, my boy, the answering mark of where the
    fetter is!

Oh! many a weary hundred years his sires that fetter
    wore,
And he has worn it since the day that him his
    mother bore;
And now, my son, it waits on you, the moment you
    are born,
The old hereditary badge of suffering and scorn!

Alas, my boy so beautiful! — alas, my love so brave!
And must your gallant Irish limbs still drag it to the
    grave?
And you, my son, yet have a son, foredoomed a
    slave to be,
Whose mother still must weep o'er him the tears I
    weep o'er thee!

57. SUCCESS

If you want to succeed in Irish business get one idea and develop it. Treat this idea like a piece of wood. Whittle away all the other deadwood ideas which will dissipate your energies and decimate your profits and stick to the single track.

A teacher once told me that the four biggest dunces in his class were the four richest men in his part of the country because they had only four ideas among them and they made themselves four fortunes whereas the bright boys, who had as many ideas in their heads as an archer has arrows in his quiver, never seemed to hit a worthwhile target. Like the old woman who lived in the shoe they had so many ideas they did not know what to do with them. They looked at the pros and cons, the ifs and buts, the whys and the wherefores, the maybes and maybe nots until each idea was but a pale ghost of its original and like its ethereal counterpart dissolved into nothingness.

One of the dullards had an idea about turf and he made a fortune out of it after the war when coal was scarce. He bought secondhand army lorries and got first class service from ex-servicemen who were just then hitting the civilian dole queues. In no time he was a millionaire and his entourage of workers became mini-millionaires in their own right.

The next fellow made a fortune out of butter which he sold at a £1 per pound. He could not get enough of it so great was the demand. So, without any great exertion on his part, he became another post-war millionaire. He was a very religious man who attributed his success to the number of pilgrimages he made to Rome and Lourdes. The first time he set out for Lourdes he never got there. He stayed over in Rome because, as he said when he got home, 'Dem Eyetalian wimmen have foine legs'.

The third chap made a fortune out of the grocery business. He started with cigarettes. When they were ten pence halfpenny a packet (old money) he sold five at a time for five pence halfpenny and made one halfpenny profit on every ten. You see, cigarettes were scarce too during the last war and he just could not be handing out tens to people. The bright boys would turn up their noses at such small pickings but our friend had only one idea — to make money slowly but surely.

Next it was the turn of matches. He split each box into two and provided cheap labour for local schoolboys. In those days a halfpenny was good money and for a halfpenny each he got schoolboys to collect the empty boxes. He would not accept them unless they were bone dry. A man of impeccable standards! For another halfpenny each he got them to empty half the matches from fifty boxes into fifty empties (for he was nothing if not generous). So for the expenditure of one penny he made a profit of fifty pennies which was the price of fifty boxes.

Nothing escaped his scythe. Next it was the turn of sweets which — you're quite right — were also scarce. He specialised in sweets which cost two pence halfpenny per half pound or six pence halfpenny per quarter and never sold anyone more than two ounces for he wanted to give everyone a fair crack of the whip. Again pickings were small — an extra halfpenny on each quarter. Farthings were in use, of course, during this period but it would be a very shortsighted customer who would insist in getting his farthing's worth. His original idea was to make a fortune out of halfpennies and how well he succeeded may be gauged from the fact that he left £50,000 (to his heirs) which in halfpennies of the old kind amounted to 24,000,000. Fair play to him, he was not above overcharging for other commodities as well for, God be good to him, he was no snob.

Dunce number four made a fortune out of blackthorn. His labour force was recruited from the bums and ne'er-do-wells who idled at street corners. He lured them from their leisure to help him with promises of free porter which they adored and plenty of fresh air which not one of them had the slightest interest in. They scoured the woods and dales of rural Ireland for their raw material and before long your man's blackthorn walking sticks were hopping off the polls of urban Teddy Boys while in Chicago's saloons his black-thorn pipes were creating smoke screens, behind which more than plug was cut. It was only when he denuded the hills and forests of his native Kerry that he stopped making money.

Anyone of the four of them could not pass an exam if it killed him. Where would they be if they had? There were many other not so bright boys (scholastically, that is) who did well. Some made fortunes out of thirst (other people's) and more made fortunes out of 'Ating' houses. Some out of guns and more out of buns. The fellow who made his money out of buns told me that he got his idea while listening to a farmer talking to his son on the morning of an Abbeyfeale calf fair and I quote:

Farmer: 'Will you ate a bun?'

Son: 'Wouldn't I ate a winda fullovum.'

Our friend supplied many windafulls and while the envious may try to crack his plate glass they'll never get near his gold plate.

Others made fortunes out of gallon sweets. There's many a farmer would mow an acre of land after a feed of gallon sweets. Gallon sweets were the making of dentists — a job that's all pull.

I know fellas who made fortunes out of bulls and others who made them out of bulldozers because the poor chaps were not good at their sums.

So, for God's sake, parents, if the kids have just one idea let them be — they could be potential millionaires but if their heads are full of ideas they'll either wind up as civil servants or teachers or hired help of some kind while chappies not half as bright will be making fortunes.

In concluding let me make a few suggestions that you could capitalise on:

1. If you are a plastics merchant start a campaign to bring back collar studs and make yourself a fortune.

2. This is for leprachauns — I know there are a few left who have not emigrated to the U.S. Why not invisibly mend broken cigars and peddle them to third class tourists at half price?

3. You're an entrepreneur. Why not persuade people who are very busy to let you do their Christmas shopping for them.

58. THE BLIND POET

Minstrel, I pray of you light!
    Your eyes are dark and your hand
Gropes at the walls left and right,
    And the rain sweeps you in from the land.

Yet light from your darkness I pray,
    Or the touch of your hand, or the sound
Of your voice at the fall of the day,
    And your blind stick tapping the ground.

I'd eat of the meal in your bag,
    Food homely and kind, and I'd taste
Of Connacht, of mountain and crag,
    And lakeland and heathery waste.

I'd learn a song at your knee
    And mine would come tender and true,
More simple, more Gaelic, maybe
    Not so bitter, remembering you.

If you taught me a hornpipe or reel,
    My heart, lighted up, would remain
Like a house in a glen to which steal
    The dancers through darkness and rain.

O Minstrel, the grain in your sack
    Never grew in these mountainy lands,
And the fiddle astride on your back
    Were dumb in less sanctified hands.

And the touch of your stick is a cure,
    And the light in your heart will not die,
For you come, and no mortal is sure
    Whether you or Love's self passes by!

59. THE COURTEOUS REPLY

One might begin with a story from County Fermanagh which seems to be typical of the cursing-contest within the last hundred years. It appears that a rate-collector, named Willis, generally expressed his displeasure at the delay in paying the rate-demands by loudly cursing the tenant. One day he called to a farmer, called Murphy, and found that he did not have the ready cash to meet his obligations. Willis began to curse him but Murphy replied in such a fluent fashion that the competitive soul of Willis was aroused. He promised Murphy that if he defeated him in a cursing-contest he would remit the rates and pay them out of his own pocket. If Willis won on the other hand, Murphy promised that he would raise the money somewhere, no matter how humiliating this admission of poverty was. The two commenced cursing and eventually Willis said:

May your hens take the disorder (the fowl-pest), your cows the crippen (phosphorosis), and your calves the white scour! May yourself go stone-blind so that you will not know your wife from a hay-stack!

To this sally Murphy retorted in the following manner and defeated his opponent:

May the seven terriers of hell sit on the spool of your breast and bark in at your soul-case!

In this interesting manner the good farmer Murphy secured a total rebate of his rates for the year.

60. IRISH ISLAND

They are now planning to send the young people into the *Gaeltacht* so that they may speak to the old people in every part of it. It is a good idea, indeed an excellent one. But a single month there won't be of much benefit; they should be a year among the old people, talking and listening to them... That's the thing that would make native speakers of the young folk; after a few years they would be apt and fluent speakers...

Everyone knows what the tide is like when it starts to flood. According as the water is rising it is spreading out and spurting into every place so that it doesn't leave a harbour or a strand, an inlet or a rock-crevice, nor any hidden bay or hole or corner that it doesn't fill. And I think the tide of Irish is beginning to fill in the self-same way.

But I suppose that I won't be able to do much to help in that matter; however I will do whatever is in my power, whether God leaves me alive for a long or a short time. I will not hold back as much as a single word of the ancient heritage of the speech that I inherited from the old people: I wouldn't have such meanness in my mind nor crankiness in my heart at this time of my life as to conceal or cloak anything I ever heard that would be of any benefit in the work. And so I am now doing my best, before the shovels throw the clay over my eyes, to leave that heritage as a legacy to the young that are growing up to take my place.

61. OPPOSITION

Some T.D.'s is the Government and some is the Opposition. The Government is to pass things to rule the country and the Opposition is to stop them. They get paid for this. The Government is bigger than the Opposition. The Opposition do not like this, and they are always saying that everything in the country is rotten and the Government saying it is grand. Then the Opposition gets bigger than the Government and the Government is the Opposition and the Opposition is the Government and the Government that was the Opposition say everything is grand that was rotten and the

Opposition that was the Government says everything is rotten that was grand which is the opposite, politicians not minding what they say. The people can say nothing, only pay the taxes.

62. BANNED

'Tailor, they have put you on the banned list.'

'Yerra, there's no end to the honours. Now what band would it be? It wouldn't be the Quarry Lane band, by any chance, would it, for that was a right good band in the days when I was in Cork. Not like those queer confraternity bands and temperance bands... Temperance bands, moyah!... Did you ever hear the like?'

'No, Tailor. I'm sorry but it isn't that kind of a band at all. The book is banned. It isn't to be sold any more.'

'Whyfor so?... Is it how they have run out of paper?'

'No. I'm afraid that that isn't the reason.'

'Well, it must be that everyone has a copy got. It won't be long now before Ireland becomes the wisest country in the whole world when they all have it read.'

'It is the law which says that it isn't to be sold any more.'

'The law! ... That explains it so... That's what you would expect from the law... You might as well be trying to hang your hat on a rainbow as expecting sense from the law... Haven't I had dealings with them myself. They only see the world upside down and back to front... But tell me, what has the law got to do with the book?'

'The Minister of Justice has appointed a board of censorship. They read all the books and then advise him whether they should be sold or not.'

'Thon amon dieul! You don't mean to tell me that they have invented another Board. Haven't we already more than enough with the Tourist Board, the Turf Board, the Pig Board, the Egg Board and the Warble Fly Board to plague us, and now you tell me they have got even another... Do you know what it is? At this rate of progress we'll soon find ourselves in the strangest position any country ever found itself. We'll wake up one morning and find that everyone in the country is either in the Government or on a board and they is no one left to govern.'

The Tailor settled the fire and hung the kettle on the hook. The other half of the banned came in with a clatter of buckets.

'The divil break your legs! Whatfor have you the kettle hanging?... 'Tis only half an hour ago since we had the dinner.'

'To cool it, woman. To cool it,' replied the Tailor to the challenge.

Ansty stands aghast, bereft, for a moment only, of speech.

'Have you ne'er a splink left? To cool it, woman. To cool it... and the serious puss on him.'

'Only following government orders, ma'am. The government decided this morning that there is to be no more sense in Ireland and in future the country has to be run on government lines. That's why I put the kettle on the fire to cool it.'

With the peremptory air of a self-appointed Kettle Unhanging Board, Ansty lifted the kettle off the hook and sallied out into the sanity of the fresh air.

'Tell me,' said the Tailor after the interruption, 'What's it all about at all?'

'The government have stopped the sale of the book because the Board think that it is "indecent".

'Indecent. Indecent!... When I was in Scotland there was a man who got a gaol sentence for indecency, and rightly so, but, in the name of God, how could a book be "indecent"?

'The Board of Censorship has decided that the book is "indecent" insofar as it is suggestive of or inciting to, sexual immorality or unnatural vice or likely in any similar way to corrupt or deprave'.

'By the mockstick of war! 'Tis like a mouthful of hot porridge . . . "sexual immoralitee", indeed! so the board read the book and that's what the poor fellows found in it so... 'Twas ever said that, search hard enough and be sure that you will find what you are looking for... The man with dark spectacles sees all the world dark.'

The Tailor poked at the sods on the hearth for a moment or two as he digested all this.

''Tis a funny state of affairs when you think of it ... The book is nothing but the talk and the fun and the laughter which has gone on for years round this fireside... Not alone this fireside but every fireside in Ireland for hundred of years past and it took our own Irish government to discover that it

95

was "sexual immoralitee"... our own elected Minister for Justice and his board of ould hairpins... Did none of them, or the Minister himself, never sit at an Irish fireside at night and listen to and join in the talk... or are they all but a pack of Dublin jackeens, aping the English.

'Many years ago there was a man came to this county to do it a great harm. He was a man by the name of Cromwell. A sour-faced divil if ever there was one. He would shoot anyone he saw smiling. Before he came Ireland was known the world over as a county of laughter and fun and sport of every kind. Cromwell came with his army to stop all that. That was a long time ago. But it looks now to me that he left a lot of descendants... Yerra, when is the next election?... You'll be down later for a piece of the night? but before you go let me have the bit of law gibberish again... suggestive to or inciting to sexual immoralitee or unnatural vice or likely in any other way to corrupt or deprave... Have I got it right... I'll be wondering in the meantime was it the story of Johnny Con's sow which incited the board to sexual immoralitee or the bit about the tourist who didn't know the difference between a bull and a cow which depraved and corrupted the Minister.'

That night the Tailor sang. He sang *The Buttermilk Lasses'* He had a new concluding verse for it.

> *Now all you young maidens,*
> *Don't listen to me*
> *For I will incite you to immoralitee*
> *Or unnatural vice or in similar way*
> *Corrupt or deprave you or lead you astray*

63. WITCH OR SAINT?

Locally, the writings of an Englishman, William West were quoted: 'An enchanter or charmer was recognised... by certain words spoken and characters or images, herbs or other things applied, (they) think they can do anything they like, the devil so deceives them, or by his action does those things which the enchanters would have done...'

Because such words were being preached, it was difficult for the peasants of rural Ireland to understand whether the power that an individual like Biddy Early had come from a demon or from God. Naturally many feared her and would have nothing to do with her.

I knew a man named Tom Hayes that lived in Barr A Geagaim about seventy years ago. Tom told the local parish priest in confession that he went to Biddy for a cure. The priest told him that as a penance he'd have to go bare-headed and bare-footed, and show himself to Father Bowler P.P. of Tulla. He had to do it. (Pat MacNamara).

My uncle Jim Minogue lived near Biddy at Kilbarron. He got a fever. People were forbidden by the Church to go to Biddy. So my grandmother would not allow Jim to be brought to her. Jim got better again. Next day after that, my mother and Biddy were beating clothes in a little stream.

'Your mother would not let Jim come near me.

Jim is better now. Your mother will come to see me next time,' she said. The next time he got bad, he died.

64. PEARSE AUTOBIOGRAPHY

There has been so much tempest in my life that the quiet places in which my childhood was spent, and the quiet voices that sounded there, seem to me sometimes not to have belonged to my life at all, but to have been part of the life of another of whom I have heard or read, or whom I have imagined: one whom I can observe with considerable detachment as the story of his days pieces itself together in my mind again, and his dreams come back to me.

And this detachment is in no wise inconsistent with a certain clarity and definiteness in the recollections of impressions and emotions. I am not sure whether it is a good thing for a man to possess, as fully as I have possessed it, the faculty of getting, as it were, outside of himself and of contemplating himself as if from a little distance.

Many of my failures have doubtless been due to the fact that my thoughts and emotions of yesterday, my ordeals and triumphs of tomorrow, have always been more to me than my deeds of today: the remembered or imagined experience more insistent than the actual. Often in a world which demands swift and ruthless action I have found myself pausing to catch some far-off sound, the echo of a long silent voice, or to anticipate some unspeakable glory of a new sunrise or moonrise. When people have been talking to me about national policies, I have been listening to the flickering of the wings of flies on a window-pane that I once knew; in the midst of military plans and organisations I have been watching myself as a child come out of a certain green gate into a certain sun-lit field; or as a lad breasting great breakers beneath the moon, striving with strong white shoulders, wet and glistening.

And continually my thoughts have gone back to the places that were first familiar to me, and my ear has heard the voices that it first heard. I will set it down to my credit, that I have never loved any place better than those old places; or any voice better than those old voices. I have been faithful to them in my heart even when I have deliberately turned my feet from them, seeking far places and far voices...

You must not think that we who love perilous adventure have not also the common affections; that we do not remember, as poignantly as you bankers and solicitors and government clerks, some fireside where our kin once gathered, some caress of a woman's or a child's hand. For myself, I have never gone out to do any difficult thing, or to face any long road of sea or land, that my heart did not yearn at the leave-taking; and I have never spent a night away from the house where my kin were that I would not have given much to be among them.

Two things have constantly pulled at cross-purposes in me: one, a deep homing instinct, a desire beyond words to be at home always, with the same beloved faces, the same familiar shapes and sounds about me; the other, an impulse to seek hard things to do, to go on far quests and fight for lost causes.

What I have written here is the only defence I shall make for myself in this book, whose object, as I plan it, is simply to record things done and thought; not to explain, or to apologise for, or to justify anything. And it may perhaps stand as a defence for many a nameless brother of the ages; for I suppose that what I have said of myself is true of many others, and has its root in some old duality in the nature of man who, born of a woman, is yet the child of God. The woman in us loves to sit by our fireside; the man in us urges us forth on divine adventures.

65. ADARE

Oh, sweet Adare! oh, lovely vale!
    Oh, soft retreat of sylvan splendour!
Nor summer sun, nor morning gale,
    E'er hailed a scene more softly tender.
How shall I tell the thousand charms
    Within thy verdant bosom dwelling,
Where, lulled in Nature's fost'ring arms,
    Soft peace abides and joy excelling!

Ye morning airs, how sweet at dawn
    The slumbering boughs your song awaken,
Or linger o'er the silent lawn,
    With odour of the harebell taken.
Thou rising sun, how richly gleams
    Thy smile from far Knockfierna's mountain,
O'er waving woods and bounding streams,
    And many a grove and glancing fountain.

Ye clouds of noon, how freshly there,
    When summer heats the open meadows,
O'er parched hill and valley fair,
    All coolly lie your veiling shadows.
Ye rolling shades and vapours grey,
    Slow creeping o'er the golden heaven,
How soft ye seal the eye of day,
    And wreath the dusky brow of even.

In sweet Adare and jocund spring
    His notes of odorous joy is breathing,
The wild birds in the woodland sing,
    The wild flowers in the vale are wreathing.
There winds the Mague, as silver clear,
    Among the elms so sweetly flowing;
There, fragrant in the early year,
    Wild roses on the banks are blowing.

66. IRELAND'S DEAD

Though my own sorrows were a rising flood
    Yet could I forget them while I drown
To think of peasant lads who give their blood
    In hillside skirmishes of no renown.

I picture them as I have seen their like
    Slow, slow, in bog and field, in stall and byre;
But hark, a voice! and they snatch up the pike
    And cry out 'Freedom,' and their hearts are
        fire!

I hear them speak as I have heard their kind:
    Low, low, yet earnest in the merriest hour;
But hark, a call! and oh! my timid mind
    Trembles to hear it answered with such power!

If every field in this dear land to me
    Be as a verse of high enduring song,
If every stream that rushes to the sea
    Be as a harp-string, passionate and strong.

'Tis that shy peasant lads in every field
    Pour their young blood until the streams are
        red —
O crimson streams! O land! what songs you yield
    As I go by you reckoning the dead!

67. MANIPULATION

True relationship does not come from manipulation. The threat 'After all I've done for you' or 'If you loved me you wouldn't leave me' of 'If you don't marry me I'll have a nervous breakdown' is sometimes the final argument which makes a person who hates hurting anyone agree to marry. It is a kind of emotional blackmail. But control by one person and submission by the other do not form the basis for the relationship of a marriage. A man who always got his own way with his mother by holding on until she got tired of saying 'no' does the same with the person he sets out to marry. And a girl who grew up with a delicate parent who was easily upset may feel guilt in refusing. Always worried about others, she prefers to please rather than follow her own wishes.

The power that a certain kind of man can exercise over the woman he wants to make his wife can be extraordinary and frightening. Outwardly correct, polite and attentive to her and her welfare but with an undefinable remoteness and emotional coldness which prevent her from getting near him as a person or learning much about him, he can nevertheless talk her into marrying him. His apparent concern can be the trap into which she falls. He can brainwash, drown her in a barrage of plausible arguments and go round and round with intellectual reasons which leave her confused, unable to think straight or to know what she feels. The engagement may be broken off, giving her a tremendous sense of freedom and of being herself again, but the danger is that if she takes him back his presence, words and assurances finally convince her that he must be right and she is wrong. His persistence overcomes her resistance. Early in marriage the terrible mistake of not listening to her own feelings comes home to her. His uncanny knack of hitting on her weak points, of knowing how and where to hurt her fully appears and is a constant subtle threat which can break a wife unless she is a woman of emotional stability, sufficiently strong and resolute to withstand and overcome.

68. THINGS DELIGHTFUL

Sweet is a voice in the land of gold,
Sweet is the calling of wild birds bold;
Sweet is the shriek of the heron hoar,
Sweet fall the billows of Bundatrore.

Sweet is the sound of the blowing breeze,
Sweet is the blackbird's song in the trees;
Lovely the sheen of the shining sun,
Sweet is the thrush over Casacon.

Sweet shouts the eagle of Assaroe,
Where the gray seas of MacMorna flow;
Sweet calls the cuckoo the valleys o'er,
Sweet, through the silence, the corrie's roar.

Fionn, my father, is chieftain old
Of seven battalions of Fianna bold;
When he sets free all the deerhounds fleet
To rise and to follow with him were sweet.

69. LAST LETTER

My Dearest Mother,

I have been hoping up to now that it would be possible to see you again, but it does not seem possible. Good-bye, dear Mother. Through you I say good-bye to 'Wow-wow', Mary, Brigid, Willie, Miss Byrne, Michael, Cousin Maggie, and everyone at St Enda's. I hope and believe that Willie and the St Enda boys will be safe.

I have written two papers about financial affairs and one about my books, which I want you to get. With them are a few poems which I want added to the poems in MS. in the bookcase.

You asked me to write a little poem which would seem to be said by you about me. I have written it, and a copy is in Arbour Hill Barracks with the other papers. Father Aloysius has taken charge of another copy.

I have just received Holy Communion. I am happy, except for the grief of parting from you.

This is the death I should have asked for if God had given me the choice of all deaths — to die a soldier's death for Ireland and for freedom. We have done right. People will say hard things of us now, but later on will praise us.

Do not grieve for all this, but think of it as a sacrifice which God has asked of me and of you.

Good-bye again, dear, dear Mother. May God bless you for your great love for me and for your great faith in me, and may He remember all that you have so bravely suffered. I hope soon to see Papa, and in a little while we shall be all together again.

'Wow-wow', Willie, Mary Brigid, and Mother, good-bye. I have not words to tell you of my love for you and home, and how my heart yearns to you all.

I will call to you in my heart at the last moment.

Your son,
Pat.

70. NEW IRELAND

They destroyed our language, all but destroyed it, and in giving us their own they cursed us so that we have become its slaves. Its words seem with us almost an end in themselves, and not as they should be, the medium for expressing our thoughts.

We have now won the first victory. We have secured the departure of the enemy who imposed upon us that by which we were debased, and by means of which he kept us in subjection. We only succeeded after we had begun to get back our Irish ways, after we had made a serious effort to speak our own language, after we had striven again to govern ourselves. We can only keep out the enemy, and all other enemies, by completing that task.

71. ACH, I DUNNO!

I'm simply surrounded by lovers,
Since Da made his fortune in land;
They're comin' in crowds like the plovers
To ax for me hand.
There's clerks and policemen and teachers,
Some sandy, some black as a crow;
Ma says ye get used to the creatures,
But, ach, I dunno!

The convent is in a commotion
To think of me taking a spouse,
And they wonder I hadn't the notion
Of taking the vows.
'Tis a beautiful life and a quiet,
And keeps ye from going below,
As a girl I thought I might try it,
But, ach, I dunno!

I've none but meself to look after,
An' marriage it fills me with fears;
I think I'd have less of the laughter
And more of the tears.
I'll not be a slave like me mother,
With six of us all in a row,
Even one little baby's a bother,
But, ach, I dunno!

There's a lad that has taken me fancy,
I know he's a bit of a limb,
And though marriage is terrible chancy,
I'd chance it with him,
He's coming tonight — oh — I tingle,
From the top of me head to me toe;
I'll tell him I'd rather live single,
But, ach, I dunno!

72. GORGE III. 1760—1820

Gorge III was divided into three parts (see Oxford History) from having too long a rein and this made him mad. He was noted for sacred societies, namely Whiteboys going around Munster in the night with their shirts hanging out, these being white at that time, knocking ditches and throwing landlords into dikes full of briars. This was to stop the landlords putting ditches round the commoners which were always grazed by all the people. Father Sheehy was tried for unrolling Whiteboys, also for murdering a man who went to America to pretend to be dead. Father Sheehy was innocent in Dublin but guilty in Clonmel where it was easy to be guilty, being the chief town of the Ascendancy in County Tipperary, now, however, noted for being the seat of the County Council, and other canned meat, also cider, girls' shoes, and greyhounds. Fr Sheehy was executed by the English, and the man he murdered came home.

The Protestants also had a sacred society called Heads of Oak from being like old oak trees. They were going around in the night time attacking the big people, also Heads of Steel attacking men in the middle for going between the landlords and the tenants.

73. FROM THE DOCK

But how shall I speak of the informer, Mr John Devany! What language should be employed in describing the character of one who adds to the guilt of perfidy to his associates the crime of perjury to his God! — the man who eating of your bread, sharing your confidence, and holding, as it were, your very purse-strings, all the time meditates your overthrow and pursues it to its accomplishment! How paint the wretch who, under pretence of agreement in your opinions, worms himself into your secrets only to betray them; and who, upon the same altar with you, pledges his faith and fealty to the same principles, and then sells faith, and fealty, and principles, and you alike, for the unhallowed Judas guerdon! Of such, on his own confession was that distinguished upholder of the British crown and government, Mr Devany. With an affrontery that did not falter, and knew not how to blush, he detailed his own participation in the acts for which he was prosecuting me as a participator. And in the evidence of a man like that — a conviction obtained upon such evidence — any warrant for a sentence depriving me of all that make life desirable or enjoyable!

He was first spy for the crown — in the pay of the crown, under the control of the crown, and think you he had any other object than to do the behests of the crown!

He was next the traitor spy, who had taken that one fatal step from which in this life there is no retrogression — that one plunge in infamy from which there is no receding — that one treachery for which there is no earthly forgiveness; and, think you, he hesitated about a perjury more or less to secure present pay and future patronage! Here was one to whom existence offers now no prospect save in making his perfidy a profession, and think you he was deterred by conscience from recommending himself to his patrons! Think you that when at a distance of three thousand miles from the scenes he professed to describe, he could lie with impunity and invent without detection, he was particular to a shade in doing his part of a most filthy bargain! It is needless to describe a wretch of that kind – his own actions speak his character. It were superfluous to curse him, his whole existence will be a living, a continuing curse. No necessity to use the burning words of the poet and say:—

'May life's unblessed cup for him
Be drugged with treacheries to the brim.'

74. GRAVESTONE

Far from the churchyard dig his grave,
On some green mound beside the wave;
To westward, sea and sky alone,
And sunsets. Put a mossy stone,
With mortal name and date, a harp,
And bunch of wild-flowers carven sharp;
Then leave it free to winds that blow,
And patient mosses creeping slow,
And wandering wings and footsteps rare
Of human creatures pausing there.

75. THE FOOL

Since the wise men have not spoken, I speak that
    am only a fool;
A fool that has loved his folly,
Yea, more than the wise men their books or their
    counting houses, or their quiet homes,
Or their fame in men's mouths;
A fool that in all his days hath done never a
    prudent thing,
Never hath counted the cost, nor recked if another
    reaped
The fruit of his mighty sowing, content to scatter
    the seed;
A fool that is unrepentant, and that soon at the
    end of all
Shall laugh in his lonely heart as the ripe ears fall
    to the reaping-hooks,
And the poor are filled that were empty,
Tho' he go hungry.

I have squandered the splendid years that the Lord
    God gave to my youth
In attempting impossible things, deeming them
    alone worth the toil.
Was it folly or grace? Not men shall judge me, but
    God,
I have squandered the splendid years:
Lord, if I had the years I would squander them
    over again,
Aye, fling them from me!
For this I have heard in my heart, that a man shall
    scatter, not hoard,

Shall do the deed of today, nor take thought of
    tomorrow's teen,
Shall not bargain or huxter with God; or was it a
    jest of Christ's
And is this my sin before men, to have taken Him
    at His word?

The lawyers have sat in council, the men with the
    keen, long faces,
And said, 'This man is a fool', and others have said,
    'He blasphemeth';
And the wise have pitied the fool that hath striven
    to give a life
In the world of time and space among the bulks of
    actual things,
To a dream that was dreamed in the heart, and that
    only the heart could hold.
O wise men, riddle me this: what if the dream
    come true?
What if the dream come true? and if millions
    unborn shall dwell
In the house that I shaped in my heart, the noble
    house of my thought?
Lord, I have staked my soul, I have staked the
    lives of my kin
On the truth of Thy dreadful word. Do not
    remember my failures,
But remember this my faith.

And so I speak.
Yea, ere my hot youth pass, I speak to my people
    and say:
Ye shall be foolish as I; ye shall scatter, not save;

Ye shall venture, your all, lest ye lose what is more
    than all;
Ye shall call for a miracle, taking Christ at His
    word.
And for this I will answer, O people, answer here
    and hereafter,
O people that I have loved shall we not answer
    together?

76. MAIRE MY GIRL

Over the dim, blue hills
Strays a wild river,
Over the dim, blue hills
Rests my heart ever.
Dearer and brighter than
Jewels and pearl
Dwells she in beauty there,
Maire my girl.

Down upon Claris heath
Shines the soft berry,
On the brown harvest tree
Droops the red cherry;
Sweeter the honey lips,
Softer the curl
Straying adown thy cheeks,
Maire my girl.

'Twas on an April eve
That I first met her,
Many an eve shall pass
Ere I forget her.
Since my young heart has been
Wrapped in a whirl,
Thinking and dreaming of
Maire my girl.

She is too kind and fond
Ever to grieve me,
She has too pure a heart
E'er to deceive me;
Were I Tyrconnel's chief,
or Desmond's Earl,
Life would be dark without
Maire my girl.

77. BEETHOVEN

Music as of the winds when they awake,
    Wailing, in the mid forest; music that raves
    Like moonless tides about forlorn sea-caves
On desolate shores, where swell weird songs and
        break
In peals of demon laughter; chords athirst
    With restless anguish of divine desires—

The voice of a vexed soul ere it aspires
With a great cry for light; anon a burst
Of passionate joy—fierce joy of conscious might,
    Down-sinking in voluptuous luxury;
Rich harmonies, full-pulsed with deep delight,
    And melodies dying deliciously
As odorous sighs breathed through the quiet night
    By violets. Thus Beethoven speaks for me.

78. CAHIRMEE FAIR

Proud he goes riding now from Cahirmee fair,
No wonder, his pockets well filled from his
      bargaining there;
One hundred, two hundred, three hundred pounds
    in red gold,
The hunter, bay gelding and colt at the highest
    price sold.

Purple and strong, O look at him riding now,
Mopping the sweat from his neck and shiny brow;
He's switching his cob just to make it prance and
      show off,
And he passes Jack Lynch of the Glen, with a
    gentleman's cough!

Jack Lynch of the Glen goes home from the fair
    as he came,

His shivery nag is half-blind and a little bit lame;
What did he ask for her? — fiver or two pound
     or one?
Take it home, Jack Lynch, and blind it and up
     with the gun!

Jack Lynch of the Glen, if you stood in here by
     the hedge
Where I'm crouching ahide, I'd tell you a tale with
     an edge,
And you'd laugh at him there in the glory and
     pride of his life,
As he makes for his farm on the hill and his high-
     born wife.

Today wherever he turned in Cahirmee fair
With his 'Hi, Dan, hi, Shawn, hi, Bill, bring it over
     here,'
What did he see, like a ghost at the horse's side,
But the rag of a woman he vowed to take home as
     his bride!

And he couldn't keep still, he couldn't, but
     slapping his horse,
Would cry 'Stand back, give it room,' and many a
     curse
Would darken his lips, and his sweaty and fiery eye
Wouldn't glance at the woman at all and she
     standing by!

And now and he riding there with his head so high,
Who can picture the sight that's dazzling and
     blinding his eye;

God knows if his horse takes fright and throws him
    down dead
'Tis a spirit in rags will be glawming the horse's
    head!

Go home, Jack Lynch, to your hard-working, child-
    bearing wife,
And up with the gun and put that poor nag out of
    life.
Ground down and broken you are, yet your house
    in the Glen
Is holy, and may it be holy for ever, Amen!

They're gone, Jack Lynch and himself, and the
    night's coming down,
And a job I'll have now to find shelter or food in
    the town;
God forgive us, 'tis many a curse on himself I
    have laid,
But sure for Jack Lynch, without call, as much
    have I prayed!

79. POBLACHT NA hEIREANN

THE PROVISIONAL GOVERNMENT
OF THE
IRISH REPUBLIC
TO THE PEOPLE OF IRELAND
1916

Irishmen and Irishwomen: In the name of God and of the dead generations from which she receives her old tradition of nationhood, Ireland, through us, summons her children to her flag and strikes for her freedom.

Having organised and trained her manhood through her secret revolutionary organisation, the Irish Republican Brotherhood, and through her open military organisations, the Irish Volunteers and the Irish Citizen Army, having patiently perfected her discipline, having resolutely waited for the right moment to reveal itself, she now seizes that moment, and, supported by her exiled children in America and by gallant allies in Europe, but relying in the first on her own strength, she strikes in full confidence of victory.

We declare the right of the people of Ireland to the ownership of Ireland, and to the unfettered control of Irish destinies, to be sovereign and indefeasible. The long usurpation of that right by a foreign people and government has not extinguished the right, nor can it ever be extinguished except by the destruction of the Irish people. In every generation the Irish people have asserted their right to national freedom and sovereignty; six times during the past three hundred years they have asserted it in arms. Standing on that fundamental right and again asserting it in arms in the face of the world, we hereby proclaim the Irish Republic as a Sovereign Independent State, and we pledge our lives and the lives of our comrades-in-arms to the cause of its freedom, of its welfare, and of its exaltation among the nations.

The Irish Republic is entitled to, and hereby claims, the allegiance of every Irishman and Irishwoman. The Republic guarantees religious and civil liberty, equal rights and equal opportunities to all its citizens, and declares its resolve to pursue the happiness and prosperity of the whole nation and of all its parts, cherishing all the children of the national equally, and oblivious of the differences carefully fostered by an alien government, which have divided a minority from the majority in the past.

Until our arms have brought the opportune moment for the establishment of a permanent National Government, representative of the whole people of Ireland and elected by the suffrages of all men and women, the Provisional Government, hereby constituted, will administer the civil and military affairs of the Republic in trust for the people.

We place the cause of the Irish Republic under the protection of the Most High God, Whose blessing we invoke upon our arms, and we pray that no one who serves that cause will dishonour it by cowardice, inhumanity, or rapine. In this

supreme hour the Irish nation must, by its valour
and discipline and by the readiness of its children
to sacrifice themselves for the common good,
prove itself worthy of the august destiny to which
it is called.

Signed on Behalf of the Provisional Government

Thomas J. Clarke

Sean Mac Diarmada　　　*Thomas Mac Donagh*
P. H. Pearse　　　　　　*Eamonn Ceannt*
James Connolly　　　　　*Joseph Plunkett*

80. ALONE

Alone all alone by the wave-washed shore
Alone in the crowded hall.
Though the hall it is gay and the waves are grand
But my heart is not there at all.
It flies far away, by night and by day,
To the times and the tides that are gone.
But I never can forget, the sweet maid I met
In the valley near Slievenamon.

It was not the grace of her queenly air,
Nor her cheek of the rose's glow,
Nor her soft black eyes, nor her flowing hair,
Nor was it her lily-white brow.
'Twas the soul of truth, and of melting ruth
And the smile like a summer dawn,

That stole my heart away, one lovely summer day
In the valley near Slievenamon.

In the festive hall, by the star-watched shore,
My restless spirit cries;
My love, oh my love, shall I ne'er see you more,
And, my land, will you ne'er uprise?
By night and by day I ever, ever pray,
While lonely my life flows on,
To see our flag unrolled, and my true love to enfold,
In the valley near Slievenamon.

SOURCES

1: MISE EIRE by P.H. Pearse translated by John M. Feehan.

2: MAIRIN DE BARRA by Sean O Coilean (1754–1817) translated by Riobard O Farachain. Taken from the paperback LOVE SONGS OF THE IRISH edited by James N. Healy. O Farachain's translation is far superior to the original Irish version.

3: From the paperback TALES FROM THE SCHOOL AROUND THE CORNER by Paddy Crosbie.

4: BELIEVE ME IF ALL THOSE ENDEARING CHARMS by Thomas Moore from the paperback LOVE SONGS OF THE IRISH edited by James N. Healy. Moore's wife's face was ruined by a skin disease shortly after they had married and she feared that she might lose his affection as a result. His reply was to write this beautiful song.

5: From a speech of the Dean of St. Pauls 1941.

6. Part of Wolfe Tone's speech from the dock.

7: From THE POEMS OF FRANCIS LEDWIDGE.

8: From the paperback THE GENTLE ART OF MATCHMAKING by John B. Keane.

9: I KNOW I'M IRISH by Brenda Yasin.

10: From the paperback THE WIND THAT ROUND THE FASTNET SWEEPS by John M. Feehan.

11: From an Irish Provincial paper.

12: MISE RAFTERI by Antoine Reachtabhra (1670–1738) translated by John M. Feehan.

13:   I MARRIED A PAPIST by Jimmy Young (Emerald Records).

14.   From CAINT AN tSEAN SAOGHAIL by Arland Ussher.

15.   News item in the SUNDAY PRESS 1979.

16.   From the paperback THE MIDNIGHT COURT by Brian Merriman. Translated by Patrick C. Power.

17.   From the paperback WITCHCRAFT IN IRELAND by Patrick Byrne.

18.   From THE POEMS OF FRANCIS LEDWIDGE. Ledwidge joined the British Army out of loyalty to his patron Lord Dunsany. He was a close friend of Daniel Corkery and I recall on one occasion Corkery saying that Ledwidge told him he should have been fighting against the British in the G.P.O. in 1916. He was killed on the Western front in 1917.

19.   From FELLOW TRAVELLERS by Brenda Yasin.

20.   From the paperback THE DIARY OF HUMPHREY O'SULLIVAN translated by Tomas de Bhaldraithe.

21.   From an Emergency Powers Order issued by the Civil Service in 1940.

22.   FORNOCHT A CHONACH TU by P. H. Pearse. Translated by John M. Feehan.

23.   From THE POEMS OF JOYCE KILMER. The famous author of the poem TREES wrote this in memory of Joseph Plunkett executed by the British in 1916.

24.   The last will of John Langley who died in Clonmel. The reference to 'Oliver's Whelp' is to Cromwell.

25. From THE POEMS OF EDMUND LEAMY.

26. From THE POEMS OF FRANCIS LEDWIDGE.

27. From the paperback TO-MORROW TO BE BRAVE by John M. Feehan.

28. From the paperback CEOLTA GAEL by Sean Og and Manus O Baoill.

29. William Orr's speech from the dock.

30. From the paperback BALLADS FROM THE PUBS OF IRELAND by James N. Healy.

31. From the paperback SEX AND MARRIAGE IN ANCIENT IRELAND by Patrick C. Power.

32. From the paperback CEOLTA GAEL by Sean Og and Manus O Baoill.

33: From the paperback SELF PORTRAIT by John B. Keane.

34. From THE POEMS OF EDMUND LEAMY.

35: From the paperback THE MAGIC OF THE SHANNON by John M. Feehan.

36. PEGGY BROWNE by the blind harpist Turlough O Carolan.

37. From the paperback QUOTATIONS FROM PEARSE edited by Proinsias Mac Aonghusa.

38. From the paperback IRISH WAKE AMUSEMENTS by Sean O Suilleabhain.

39. From the paperback BALLADS FROM THE PUBS OF IRELAND by James N. Healy. Song written by William Kenealy.

40: From the paperback THE COMIC HISTORY OF LIMERICK by Paddy Lysaght.

41: From THE POEMS OF EDMUND LEAMY.

42: From the paperback BLESS ME FATHER by Eamon Kelly.

43: From the paperback THE THIRD BOOK OF IRISH BALLADS by Maureen Jolliffe.

44: Proclamation of Loyalty to the British King.

45: From THE POEMS OF EDMUND LEAMY.

46: From an Irish Newspaper 1940.

47: From THE POEMS OF SIR WILLIAM BUTLER.

48: From the paperback THE MERCIER BOOK OF IRISH RECORDS by Padraic O'Farrell.

49: By Mrs. O'Donovan Rossa. While her husband was imprisoned in Portland she sent him a picture of their baby born a week after his conviction and never seen by him. It was returned by the Governor.

50. Written by the novelist Edith Sommerville referring to the New Irish Government under W.T.Cosgrave.

51: From THE PRINCIPLES OF FREEDOM by Terence MacSwiney.

52: From THE POEMS OF EDMUND LEAMY.

53: From the paperback STORIES OF LAHY THE LIAR by Myler Magrath.

54: From a speech of Tim Healy in the English House of Commons, February 1880.

55: From CAINT AN tSEAN SAOGHAIL by Arland Ussher.

56: THE IRISH MOTHER IN THE PENAL DAYS by John Banim.

57: From the paperback HOW TO BE A SUCCESSFUL IRISH BUSINESSMAN by Michael Keane.

58. TO RAFTERY by Daniel Corkery.

59: From the paperback THE BOOK OF IRISH CURSES by Patrick C. Power.

60: From the paperback THE MAN FROM CAPE CLEAR by Conchur O Siochain. Translated by Riobard Breatnach.

61: From the paperback THE COMIC HISTORY OF IRELAND by Edmund J. Delaney & J.M. Feehan.

62: From the paperback THE TAILOR AND ANSTY by Eric Cross.

63: From the paperback THE STORY OF BIDDY EARLY by Meda Ryan.

64: From the paperback THE HOME LIFE OF PADRAIG PEARSE by Mary Brigid Pearse.

65: ADARE by Gerald Griffin.

66: From THE POEMS OF DANIEL CORKERY.

67: From the paperback TO HAVE AND TO HOLD by Tony Baggot.

68: From THE POEMS OF GEORGE SIGERSON.

69: From the paperback THE HOME LIFE OF

PADRAIG PEARSE by Mary Brigid Pearse.

70: From the paperback THE PATH TO FREEDOM by Michael Collins.

71: From the paperback PERCY FRENCH AND HIS SONGS by James N. Healy.

72: From the paperback THE COMIC HISTORY OF IRELAND by Edward J. Delaney and John M. Feehan.

73: STEPHEN JOSEPH MEANEY, speech from the dock.

74: A GRAVESTONE by William Allingham.

75: From the paperback QUOTATIONS FROM PEARSE edited by Proinsias MacAonghusa.

76: MAIRE MY GIRL by John Keegan Casey.

77: BEETHOVEN by John Todhunter.

78: CAHIRMEE FAIR by Daniel Corkery.

79: DECLARATION OF REPUBLIC 1916.

80: THE VALLEY NEAR SLIEVENAMON by Charles Kickham.